water

almost enough for everyone

by stephanie ocko
illustrated with photographs and diagrams

Atheneum Books for Young Readers

The quote on page 64 is from *To Shoot Hard Labour* by Keithlyn B. Smith and Fernando C. Smith. Edan's Publishers, published in Scarborough, Ontario, Canada, 1986; page 63.

Atheneum Books for Young Readers
An imprint of Simon & Schuster Children's Publishing Division
1230 Avenue of the Americas
New York, New York 10020

Library of Congress Cataloging-in-Publication Data
Ocko, Stephanie.
 Water : almost enough for everyone / by Stephanie Ocko.
  p. cm.
 Includes biographical references and index.
 ISBN 0-689-31797-2
 1. Droughts—Juvenile literature. 2. Water-supply—Juvenile literature. [1. Droughts.
2. Water Supply.} I. Title.
QC929.25.025 1995
363.3'492—dc20   94-34743

BOOK DESIGN BY LAURA HAMMOND HOUGH

The text of this book is set in Granjon

FIRST EDITION

Printed in the United States of America

10 9 8 7 6 5 4 3 2 1

Contents

Drought in a Small Town: Redding, Iowa

The hot October sun slants across the golden rolling fields of southern Iowa. A lone pheasant struts its hothouse plumage across the road, then flies low over the stiff brush stubble of the combed rows of harvested corn. Red lights flashing, the orange school bus waits for a couple of kids to cross the road. They swing their lunch boxes and trade insults with a boy who leans out a bus window.

The space that Redding, Iowa, occupies on the highway takes less than a minute to drive through. The only thing that might catch your eye is the Texaco station, where farmers hang out on slow days to chew the fat and talk about the weather. Set back from the road are big white houses under spreading green trees, which, along with a church with a tall white steeple, comprises the town of Redding, home to ninety-four people. They have a mayor and a post office. The general store closed in 1976.

Six thousand miles away in the middle of the Pacific Ocean, cold surface water replaced warm surface water a year ago, and Redding, Iowa, was declared a drought disaster area.

It hasn't really rained here for two years. An occasional thunderstorm rips through, but when the sun comes out again, it immediately absorbs the puddles and shrinks the ponds into tiny pools, leaving the cattle and horses little to drink.

Of all natural disasters, drought is the strangest, because psychologically it is easy to forget as soon as the rains come. "It looks normal," says Dick Snethen, the mayor, "but it's not." His trees are laden with apples; the cool green lawn waits to be cut. Growing things greedily absorb whatever moisture they can get. Even with the soil extremely dry a few inches down and with only a tiny bit of rain, farmers took in fifty bushels of corn per acre this season in 1989. But only five miles north, the yield was 150 bushels

Corn still grows during drought, like this in Morgan County, Alabama, but it is short and sparse, and the ears are not big enough to eat. National Oceanic and Atmospheric Administration.

per acre. That was because it rained normally there. The strange islands of high and low pressure zones created by the cooling of the Pacific Ocean got stuck over Iowa, and it rained all around, but not in Redding. "If Mother Nature'd turned on the spigot, everything would be all right," says Snowball Hanks, a farmer, at the Texaco station.

But the problem is very serious: the aquifers are dry. Of forty wells, thirty-eight have dried up. "One day I turned on the spigot and nothing came out," says Jerry Overholser, who works at the Texaco garage. He rolls a truck tire into the garage until it

Redding Mayor Dick Snethen delivers mail in the mornings, then works on creating a tractor out of spare parts for competition in a tractor pull.

tumbles on its side, shooting dirt out from under it. "You don't *know* the wells are dry until they're dry," he says.

The lack of moisture in the soil raises the surface temperature, which, combined with the dry warm ground, makes any amount of rain evaporate more quickly than it can accumulate. So drought goes round and round.

Snethen says that everyone in Redding is used to occasional drought and conserves water. "But this is the worst thing that has ever happened," he says. The town, he says, has survived a tornado, several snowstorms, and a plague of locusts.

call in the national guard

By the summer of 1989, Snethen and the leaders of five other small towns in the area appealed to their state senators for help. The governor called in the National Guard. The Guardsmen set up two huge tanks outside an empty former schoolhouse, and trucked in water from neighboring communities for the citizens of Redding and the five other towns. Ladies in Redding baked the Guardsmen casseroles and apple pies and brought cold drinks and hot coffee in thermos jugs to the old schoolhouse.

By the end of the summer, the state had run out of money to pay the National Guard. The governor appealed to Washington, and the U.S. Army Corps of Engineers rumbled into Redding in huge Army trucks carrying water that they hosed into the tanks.

twenty-two gallons

Each person was allowed the government-regulation twenty-two gallons of water per day, what some city dwellers use to take a

Redding's former schoolhouse, now empty, became the site for the water tanks when the U.S. Army Corps of Engineers delivered water for the town. Townspeople came in their pickups, siphoned off their daily twenty-two gallons per person, then hosed it into their wells at home.

morning shower. The average American uses about sixty gallons a day. Each week, families drove their pickups to the schoolhouse tanks. There they hooked up the hose to their portable water tanks and filled them, on the honor system, then drove home and put the water into their wells to be pumped through their pipes.

Twenty-two gallons is not a lot of water. Peggy Over-holser's daughter celebrated her sixteenth birthday in the middle of the summer with a big party. Usually she washed her long hair every other day. But for her birthday she washed it two days in a row. In the middle of the party, the Overholsers ran out of water. Peggy's mother had to jump into the pickup, drive down to the water tanks, hose in some water for a refill, then drive back, and dump it into the well.

Most families in Redding doubled up on baths, sometimes stretching one bathtub full of water to accommodate three family members. The bathwater, which was only a little soapy, could then be used to water the lawn and flowers, and wash the car.

overworked wells

In some areas wells go dry because farmers use the water supply to irrigate crops. But that isn't the case here. It's just that indoor plumbing, running water, washing machines, and improved pumps have put so much pressure on the water supply that, with drought, it simply gave out. This isn't happening just in Redding, Iowa, either: Better pumping systems all over the world are too efficient for the old wells from which they draw water.

Cindy Snethen, the mayor's wife, had just finished preparing eight apple pies that she would freeze for dessert for her family for the fall. This year she had to wash the apples in a little water in a basin, and keep the water to wash the potatoes she was planning to have for dinner that night. "A friend came in from Omaha last month," she remembered, her voice rising at the recollection of the horror, "and she was standing at the sink washing the potatoes under the *running* water, till we said, 'No! No! You can't *do* that here!'"

Everyone in Redding and in the surrounding small towns has had to deal with the problem of when to flush the toilet. Cindy says, "A banker told me he tells his family, 'If it's yellow, let it mellow; if it's brown, flush it down.' We're all in this together, whether you're a banker or on welfare. Everybody in our town sticks together anyway. If a family is having a dispute, we all share in it. If someone dies, we all mourn."

tiny towns can get lost

By the end of the summer it was clear that it was never going to rain enough to fill the wells. The ground can get remoisturized if it rains during the period between the harvest and the winter freeze. That way, when it rains again in the spring, the damp soil will absorb the rain, which then seeps into the aquifers. But it stayed dry.

So Dick Snethen and leaders from four neighboring towns formed a union to see if they could get some help. They met at the Lions' Club in Diagonal, one of the towns, to devise a strategy for interesting authorities in their problem. Then they took it to the bigger town of Creston and the Southern Iowa Rural Water Association (SIRWA), a nonprofit company that sells water. Redding and its neighbors needed piped water.

Even though it's only about a twenty-minute drive away, Creston was one of the towns that had received a lot of rain. It also had a huge reservoir, Lake Twelve Mile, and was building another one, Lake Three Mile. Creston was floating in water.

In his office, SIRWA Executive Director Earl Hanthorn ran his hand across a big wall map to show the weird rain patterns. They ranged from none in Redding to a little above Redding to completely normal above that. "No one really knows why," he said.

Hanthorn explained that a year ago they considered a project that would take seven years to build in which they would lay underground water pipes from Creston south to the tiny towns. "We shortened that to a five-year project early this year. Now it's for *tomorrow*."

the pipeline

On the map he points to a big yellow line from Creston that branches into smaller feeder lines that, like life-giving arteries, will bring water to about five thousand people in seven counties. Families of four would pay about fifty dollars a month for about sixty gallons per person per day.

Raising the money from state and federal grants to install the system was not easy. "The state says, 'Don't spend the money at the rural level on less than 2,500 population, because if we wait long enough, they'll die out,'" Hanthorn says. "And the feds aren't any more sensitive. They have to spread their funds around the whole country, and they say, 'Well, maybe there's another state that needs it more.' The little guy gets forgotten."

Back in Redding, with piped water at least a year away, Dick Snethen realized the town would have to do something to keep the water tanks from freezing over the winter. So he and leaders from the other towns fixed up an abandoned Ford showroom in Redding to house their tanks. "It's hard to fight city hall," he said.

water for the animals

Rainwater that collected in ponds was the only source of water for the cattle and horses. The Snethens didn't keep cattle. The only animal they had, aside from a couple of friendly cats, was a horse, which was Leigh Ann Snethen's love. Leigh Ann, who was a senior in high school, had had him since she was ten. She was so attached to him she wouldn't let her two younger brothers, Travis and Joe, go near him. As the drought settled into Redding, the pond out in back of the Snethens' house got smaller and smaller.

hard choices

One dry, dusty, hot afternoon in August, Leigh Ann and her father stood by the shed and looked at the tiny pond and at the thin figure of the horse. Leigh Ann had to decide. The family was about to go to Oregon for a two-week vacation. Nowhere was there any possibility of rain; and if they left their horse to eat the spare and dry grass and to drink in the shrinking pond, they knew when they came back that they would have a dead horse.

"Sell him," said Leigh Ann softly. Her father, who had fought in the Vietnam War and come back to Redding to raise his family in the safest place he knew, understood the pain in his daughter's voice. "We can always buy a new one when the drought is over," he said.

After their vacation, Leigh Ann decided to go to college at the University of Idaho and study agriculture—not to become a farmer, but to understand farming and all its problems, and how to deal with water shortages and drought and animals who were helpless even if they were cared for by loving owners.

Across the highway on Dale Walkup's farm, the choice to sell his cattle was an economic one. "I started out the summer by moving my cattle from one pond to another," he said, "wherever there was water to drink. In the next field, the pond was relatively full because the owner didn't have any cattle. But by the end of the summer, her pond was almost dry, too. I had the choice of sending the cattle to another farm north of here to graze and drink until the drought was over. But the selling price of cattle was high, so I sold the herd. I can always buy cattle again when it looks wetter," he said.

a hundred years ago

Walkup, also a Vietnam veteran and the father of three, is a fourth-generation Redding farmer. In 1900, Redding had a population of three hundred. Many of them were prosperous farmers who loaded their bushels of corn or apples or jugs of milk or bleating cattle or squealing pigs onto the train that clanged into town amid bursts of steam. Merchants, bankers, two physicians, lawyers, and newspaper editors worked in brick buildings around the town square, and ate dinner at one of two plush hotels. Their kids went to the school where today the water tanks are stored.

But world wars, drought, and the loss of the railroad to trucks and cars reduced the town to its current population of nine-

The Redding High School (old building) graduating class of 1906. Back row, standing left to right: Walter J. Stanton, (Superintendent) Elder Baird. Middle row: Winnie Abarr, Grace Bryan, Anna Grayson. Seated: Ivan Hoffman, Blanch Bernard, Archie Mekemson. Redding, Iowa, Centennial Celebration, July 10–11, 1982.

ty-four. Now the town square is a playground, and you have to hunt around in the dry grass to find the railroad tracks. What was once a busy railroad stop is now only a weedy field. In the middle, an abandoned farmhouse leans dangerously to the right.

the worst drought scenario

Most of the Great Plains and Midwestern states take their water from the huge aquifer named the Ogallala, which, because of changed rain patterns and overuse, is dangerously low. What's happened in Redding is coming up for a lot of other towns.

What would happen to Redding residents if an extreme drought extended over several years? For farmer Dale Walkup, it would mean changing what he does. "What my father told me is what I'll tell my kids if they choose to be farmers: study something else as a backup," he says. His backup is accounting. "Worst case, I'd go to a city and get a job," he says.

One farmer's answer to the drought is raising fowl—chickens or turkeys—which don't require a lot of water. Not far from Redding are factories that process eggs for cake mixes and grow chickens for Campbell's soups. "Never," says Walkup. "You have to have so many birds to make a profit, they take over your life. Besides, I'd have to divorce my wife before I kept birds."

His wife, Sharon, smiles and rocks their two-week-old son. "I always say farming is a worry. But he says it's a challenge," she said.

"I like the life," said Walkup.

the very worst drought scenario

With Redding about to rely on Creston for its water, what would happen if, in an extreme drought, *Creston's* water dried up?

Mark Duben, an engineer with SIRWA, says the climate would not change overnight. "We'd build more reservoirs," he claims. "There's always going to be *some* amount of rain. The other possibility is that some people would leave the area and the demand for water would go down." Many people migrated to California during the 1930s drought.

the priority list

The state of Iowa owns all the water in the state. If Iowa were in the grips of an extreme drought, the governor would sign into effect a priority water list, which would alert citizens that water was greatly restricted. At the top of the priority list are hospitals, homes with small children, and the chronically ill; at the bottom of the list are communities in neighboring states.

"I just can't imagine we wouldn't have time to plan for an extreme drought," Duben repeats. "It's not going to be the Sahara Desert overnight."

poisons

During a drought, the land on top of the aquifers becomes dry and cracked, even if grass still grows out of it. Behind the Snethens' house, Dick maneuvers a crooked stick into a deep crack. The six-foot-long stick all but disappears into the ground. "Look how deep that crack is," he says. "*Anything* can get into that."

Farmers use herbicides and pesticides to kill weeds and

bugs to enhance their crops. The chemicals collect in the ground. With regular rainfall, they disperse and run off into ponds and rivers or even into aquifers. Then they are diluted enough not to hurt anyone.

the rains come

In the early spring of 1990, the rains came to Redding, Iowa. They came suddenly and steadily. Rain dripped off roof gutters and ran down drainpipes and rushed in torrents along the gutters of the highway. The dry land formed gulleys, then turned into mud.

When the rains came back to Redding, the chemicals that had been trapped in the ground by the drought were released in the soil and immediately seeped into the aquifers.

"Babies are getting sick," said Cindy Snethen on the phone one day after a big rain. "I just heard of a four-year-old being air-lifted out to Des Moines to the hospital with an unexplained virus," she said. "The rains came, all right. It rained for days and nights. The wells are full, but we're afraid to use them. When I boil my water, there's a terrible brown residue around the pot. What can that be? We hear that the federal health inspectors are coming in to check the quality of the water."

The health inspectors found nothing wrong with the drinking water, but Cindy didn't trust their report. She and other families continued to boil their water for at least twenty minutes before they were satisfied it was safe to drink. They even felt bathing in it was dangerous, and took showers instead of baths.

No one knows how people would react if a severe drought seriously restricted clean, drinkable water. Would neighbor fight neighbor for a bucketful at a public well? Or would everyone pull together as people in Redding have done, staying tough against all odds?

In church in Redding one Sunday, Ann Walkup delivered a sermon. Praying for rain might not bring it, she said, because God works randomly, and this keeps us alert. "Wouldn't it be easier if God gave instant approval for good deeds and instant punishment for bad ones?" She laughs. "But God doesn't work that way. And

At Redding's church, parish-ioners take turns giving sermons on Sundays.

isn't it lucky? How else would I deserve such beautiful grandchildren?" she asks, modestly. "Not knowing the future keeps us on our toes."

It's green now in Redding. Trees are laden with apples, the grass is thick, the corn that blows in the wind is healthy and tall. Leigh Ann Snethen is getting ready for college; Travis is trying out for the football team; and Joe is working on plans to build his parents a swimming pool.

Dick and Cindy sit on their porch and look across the sloping fields. "It's green now, " said Cindy, "but that doesn't mean anything."

Dick agrees. "The weathermen are predicting extended drought here for the next ten years. We're ready for anything, I guess, except an earthquake. But I'm sure we could handle that, too."

2 Drought: Nothing New under the Sun

From the records of earth's past climates, we know that droughts have been around for a long time, that they come and go, and that they are not *directly* the result of global warming. However, in a climate that is changing, droughts might occur where they have never occurred before. If global temperatures are higher, droughts might develop faster.

Drought is one of those things that no one can agree on, but everyone knows it when they are in it: water is scarce. That can affect communities in ways ranging from being unable to water lawns to being forced to migrate to another place to live. Sociologists say that in extreme drought, people have three choices: adapt, migrate, or die.

when is it drought?
when is it just dry?

One of the problems with drought is that it is slow, hidden, and quiet. Flash floods, hurricanes, earthquakes, tornadoes, blizzards come and go quickly. But drought is like some prehistoric monster creeping on its belly through an underground tunnel. Its long tongue flicks out, sucking up water, then it lies there, its white eyes glowing in the dark. Above, the ground dries up, plants wither and

During the Dust Bowl in the American Midwest in the 1930s, farmers clung desperately to their land, hoping it would rain tomorrow. In this photo taken after a dust storm in Kansas, a farmer and his son dig away the dry soil from their fence posts. National Oceanic and Atmospheric Administration.

die, leaves turn brittle and drop, people wring water out of every available source.

Drought can't be predicted, although climatologists are working to identify what factors are likely to bring it about. Some satellites can actually measure the amount of moisture in the soil, which is a clue to the beginning of a drought. And a change in the water temperature in the Pacific Ocean, called the El Niño event, causes droughts in certain places.

The hard thing about drought in its early stages is knowing that it is there. But even when it is established, psychologists have found in a study of the American Midwest and Australia that farmers tend to believe the drought will end this year, and that it wasn't as bad as previous droughts, and they will not move because of it.

In the great drought of the American Midwest in the 1930s, for example, a lot of farmers denied that there was one. They were called the "Tomorrow People," because they were sure it would rain tomorrow. Newspapers put predictions of rain in the headlines, even if it was only a sprinkle.

Lack of rain wasn't the only problem, however. A lot of farmers had abused their land growing cash crops for a quick profit. Year after year, farmers planted the same crop in the same fields. The land was not allowed to lie fallow, and the soil became exhausted. Fierce hot winds roiled up the dry topsoil and gathered it into clouds that moved across the sky in black waves. People boarded up their windows and prayed for rain.

Small animals were affected, too. Hundreds of rabbits ran wild desperately looking for water. Farmers, carrying sticks, would form lines and march into the middle of them, killing them for food to feed their own families or to sell in town. Spiders multiplied and moved inside houses to get something to eat. Some were

A dust storm bears down on a farm in Kansas during the drought in 1936. The "dust" is dried topsoil. It pelted houses like rain, and anyone caught in it was blinded and choked.
National Oceanic and Atmospheric Administration.

small and poisonous, others were just large. Ultimately, most families packed their goods onto their cars and trucks and drove west to California.

drought is not always a calamity

Scientists identify different kinds of drought, and point out that drought is a calamity only if a community can't deal with it. If drought strikes in a community where there are already problems—economic, political, medical, agricultural—the drought will cause a crisis. But in a healthy community, drought will cause people to come up with new solutions to water problems.

types of drought

The U.S. Geological Service defines the types of drought as follows:

- *Meteorological:* It simply doesn't rain.
- *Agricultural:* More serious; the subsoil is dry, and the roots of plants are water-starved. Cornfields droop, and cattle range farther in search of grass and water.
- *Hydrological:* The water sources are low. In extreme cases, wells run dry, and water spigots just cough air when you turn them on.
- *Sociological:* A lot of people suffer because of meteorological and hydrological drought. Often they are forced to migrate to other countries, where they become environmental refugees.
- *Legislative:* When the distribution of water is imposed by law, some feel they are unjustly cheated out of the water they need.

think of a space capsule

Imagine that you are in a spaceship on a mission that will take a year. You have to carry with you everything that you will need in that time, because there will be no place to stop for supplies. Your food has been flash-frozen and packaged in small bags, and you have enough for a year. But water is heavy: one gallon weighs more than eight pounds, and the average use is about sixty gallons a day. Even if you cut back your use to fifty gallons a day, that means four hundred pounds of water per person per day. If you have a crew of five people, that's a *ton* of water to carry.

As yet, water cannot be chemically manufactured, so you will have to take a small amount, distribute it fairly to your crew, and recycle it. You can't afford to lose a drop.

The earth does the same thing, as if it were a closed capsule on a mission through space. All of the water now on earth is all we have and all we will ever have. Most of our water is stored in the oceans (97.4 percent) and is salty. Only 2.6 percent of the water on earth is fresh. And it is all constantly recycled.

the water cycle

The process starts in the ocean. The heat of the sun evaporates the water and draws it up as moisture to form clouds. Winds carry the clouds over land, where, with the help of the sun, they collect the moisture given off by man, animals, and vegetation, called transpiration and the moisture from water in surface reservoirs, rivers, and lakes, called evaporation. This combination of evaporation and transpiration is called *evapotranspiration*. The clouds give this collected moisture back to the land as rain or snow.

runoff

The water that winds up as soil moisture, in porous rock channels (aquifers), or in lakes, reservoirs, ponds, and rivers is called *runoff*. Some runoff goes back to the ocean. Runoff is the difference between the precipitation that the clouds send down and the moisture that is lost in evapotranspiration, when the sun absorbs it.

In very hot climates, the sun evaporates a lot of water that would be runoff. It takes it not only from lakes and ponds, but actually evaporates the falling rain or snow. Antigua, a sunny

water: almost enough for everyone

THE WATER CYCLE

N. J. Wylie.

island in the tropical Caribbean, for example, gets 50 percent more rainfall than average, but has only 31 percent more runoff because the sun is so strong.

It rains an average of about thirty inches all over the earth every year, which means that some places get much more than thirty inches, and others get only a trace. Parts of Central America and India, for example, get almost 400 inches (1,000 centimeters) of rain a year.

The renewable freshwater—that is, all the water stored in the ground and in lakes, rivers, and surface reservoirs in the United States—amounts to between two and thirteen million gallons per person per year. As noted earlier, the average American uses about sixty gallons per day.

new water

The amazing thing about earth's freshwater is that most of it has been used somewhere before. An ancient Roman might have taken a bath in the water you used to brush your teeth this morning.

Some people have considered towing icebergs from the poles to increase the supply of fresh water. It's one thing to get the ship and tow an iceberg, but what do you do with it once it's in the harbor? How do you collect the freshwater? How do you keep it from freezing your own coastline? If it melts too fast, will it flood your beaches?

in the hands of the winds

The critical thing about our water cycle is that it depends on clouds, and clouds are at the mercy of the winds. This means earth's water distribution system is not the same everywhere.

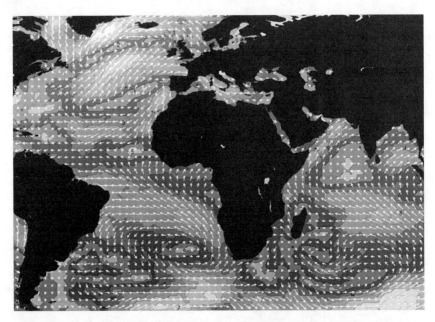

As the earth rotates on its axis, winds over the oceans follow steady paths. Sailors call them the trade winds. In the Atlantic Ocean, winds blowing out of the northern hemisphere meet winds blowing up from the southern hemisphere. They meet at the equator and blow toward the west. NASA Headquarters, Earth Sciences and Applications Division.

deserts

Some places never get enough clouds carrying precipitation. It does rain in the Sahara Desert, for example, but very little. In some places, it rains only once every seven years. But climate systems change. Twenty-five hundred years ago, the Sahara was green and fertile. Farmers planted barley and kept cattle that grazed in green fields. Villagers wove red and yellow cloth that they traded in the marketplaces.

Today archaeologists find their artwork on rock faces and hundreds of artifacts left from their lives, some of them exposed by the wind, lying on top of the sand like toys left over from a day at the beach. Sometime in the past it stopped raining. Crops died, wells dried up, and people packed their goods on their donkeys, herded together their cattle, and moved south or to the coasts.

Evidence shows that the sands of the Sahara were created, at least in part, by man: traders and the people who lived in the

A camel and cattle painted on a cave wall in the Sahara Desert, at Sefar, Tassili n'Ajjer, Algeria, between 4,500 and 7,000 years ago. Camels can travel for about a month without taking water. They do not store water in their hump—they store it throughout their body. But they keep their water losses from breathing, urinating, and sweating to a minimum; and their volume of blood plasma does not change. Cattle use four times as much water as camels. They must drink frequently, and they require more because they use it not only to rehydrate but to cool their systems.

Sahara cut down trees for fuelwood, and for charcoal to smoke meat. Acacia trees, which are adapted to semiarid climates, were leveled a century ago by traders and merchants who collected its sap, called gum arabic, which is used in glues, perfumes, and a variety of other products manufactured and sold in Europe and the Middle East.

Trees provide shade, which preserves whatever moisture is in the soil. More important, trees absorb carbon dioxide (CO_2) during photosynthesis and breathe out oxygen. Moisture or water vapor is released with oxygen. This moisture attracts rain.

Traders have been crossing the Sahara Desert in camel caravans for centuries. Over the years they have built wells wherever there was water underground. This modern-day trader in the Sahara Desert in Algeria brings up water in a small pot like those used hundreds of years ago. In the background, his camels stock up on water. National Oceanic and Atmospheric Administration.

With the trees gone, large animals, except camels and cattle, also went. Lions, which were once abundant in North Africa, retreated to the more humid East Africa. Ostriches, which hunters killed for their plumes to be used on hats, also left the Sahara for East Africa. Today the Sahara is a vast ocean of sand and rocks, its hazy expanse broken by occasional craggy, hostile mountains. The only people you meet are Bedouins, wrapped against the wind and sun, riding their camels from oasis to oasis to replenish their water.

in the hands of man

Los Angeles, one of the major cities of the world, sits on arid land, watered by an ingenious system of canals and aqueducts. Without California's water distribution system, there would be no Los Angeles. It is only one example of how humans can create systems that take water from where there is too much and put it where there is not enough.

Most cities build reservoirs to store rainwater, then purify it into drinking water. But tons of earth and hundreds of acres are disturbed when reservoirs are built. They are also expensive, and must be cleaned out from time to time. In a hot climate, the sun evaporates the exposed water. Some communities in hot climates pump water underground and store it in the aquifers.

Many rural areas depend completely on wells and pumps to bring up water that has been stored in aquifers. Big cities like New York City rely on a combination of lakes and reservoirs to hold the water that is sent to millions of New Yorkers by way of underground pipes and pumping stations.

In many parts of the world, windmills like this one in Venezuela drive a pump that brings up water from an aquifer. It is an inexpensive way of providing water for cattle in remote fields. Credit: National Oceanic and Atmospheric Administration.

aquifers

Aquifers are like underground rivers. Millions of years ago, during the Triassic Era, when the earth and oceans were forming into the landmasses that we now know, rainwater seeped into sand and lime deposits. Over the years, this sand and lime formed into sandstone and limestone. The water was trapped in cavities inside.

Many aquifers have two stories. The lower level is called a fossil aquifer, because it is compressed too deep within the earth for rainwater to reach it. In Libya, a country in the Sahara Desert, engineers are tapping into a fossil aquifer beneath the desert and have built pipes to carry the ancient water to cities several hundred miles away. The project will cost billions of dollars.

The upper aquifer level follows the rise and fall of the layer of rock in which it is embedded and receives runoff from above, so is constantly recharged with water. In some areas this freshwater lies only a few feet below the surface. The depth of an aquifer

At an oasis in Tunisia, northern Africa, a farmer adjusts the flow of water in an irrigation ditch. The water will soak into the planting beds on the left where the farmer has sown some crops. The date palms that grow at most oases thrive because they are anchored by dozens of roots that go down as deep as twenty feet into the earth, where there is more moisture. National Oceanic and Atmospheric Administration.

becomes important only when people dig wells for their houses. The best kind of well is deep enough so that the water is not contaminated by surface pollutants like car grease and laundry detergents, but not so deep that drilling is expensive.

During the drought of the early 1990s in California, farmers had to rely on the water in aquifers. In some areas, they pumped the water out so fast, aquifers collapsed. When an aquifer collapses, the ground above sinks. Once it has collapsed, it cannot be restored.

People who live in rural areas usually know where their water comes from. In drought, they dig deeper wells, build more reservoirs, or lay pipes from lakes or rivers. But in cities, most people aren't aware of their water sources. During a drought, the only options they have are to conserve water and make sure their neighbors conserve water, too; or they buy water in bottles.

When you turn on the tap, where does your water come from?

Weather: A Case of Climate Change

*Thunderstorms, hurricanes, flash floods, and volca-*noes only hint at the energy that the earth can gather up and shoot out. Winds in thunderheads, sucked up from the heated surface of the earth, reach more than a hundred miles an hour inside the cloud; and the terrific force of the swirling arms of a hurricane mixes up land and sea in a jumble of water and soil. Volcanoes explode with only the slightest forewarning, and sometimes eruptions continue for years, as at Kilauea in Hawaii.

The earth's weather is an enormously complex collection of systems in which everything, from the atmosphere to deep ocean currents, from the fall of raindrops in the middle of the sea to the sweep of the orbit of the moon, is interconnected. The main driver of the earth's energy is the sun. It provides the heat that powers the wind that draws up moisture from the ocean to form the clouds.

meteorology and climatology

Although meteorologists cannot predict drought, they usually can predict local weather events like thunderstorms. But thunderstorms might be part of bigger weather systems that stretch around the world. These bigger systems affect where droughts will occur.

Figuring out how to create models from which to predict global weather is the work of climatologists. They use information collected from satellites, weather balloons, ocean buoys, monitors on ships and mountaintops, planes flying through the upper atmos-

Cumulus clouds like these develop quickly into cumulonimbus clouds, or thunderheads. These storm clouds suck up hot surface air at speeds clocked at between twenty and ninety miles an hour inside the cloud. Traveling as fast as seventy miles an hour across an area, thunderheads shoot rain down at thirty-five miles an hour. NASA Headquarters, Earth Sciences and Applications Division.

phere, and space probes. Then they log the data into high-speed computers and try to figure out exactly why, for example, the drought in the American Midwest in 1988 was caused by a cooling of the surface waters in the eastern Pacific Ocean, thousands of miles away.

the only thing certain is change

The major discovery that climatologists have made since they have been collecting data in about 1970 is that the earth's climate is undergoing major changes. More and more, what was normal is replaced by the abnormal. It rains more in some places, hardly at all in others; fierce storms leave some areas floating in floodwaters, other areas in drought.

What are the causes?

In this climatologist's whodunit, clues are everywhere. From the air and on the sea, in the atmosphere, in the earth, and under the ocean, climatologists have amassed a multitude of clues.

el niño

Every so often (exactly how often is not certain—three years? seven years? randomly?) warm water gathers near the equator in the eastern Pacific. Usually the steady and unchanging trade winds keep things moving at the equator. Blowing down from the northern hemisphere and up from the southern hemisphere, the winds meet at the equator. Here they both blow toward the west. This drives the warm ocean currents toward the west.

But some years the trade winds are not very strong, and the ocean currents at the equator are weak. The ocean currents can't resist the force of the warm Pacific water. This warm Pacific water moves toward the east.

This is the famous El Niño, or little baby, named by fishermen who live along the coasts of Peru and Ecuador, in South America, and who first noticed that the winds changed and it rained a lot around Christmas.

But how could a little El Niño be responsible for weather changing around the world?

This is where the detectives worked overtime.

Nutrients, microscopic plants called algae, live in the deep cold waters of the oceans. Normally, they rise to the surface with the upwelling of the cold water. Here they are eaten by tiny plants called phytoplankton, which are eaten by zooplankton, which are tiny animals. Fish eat the plankton, fishermen catch the fish, sell it to people who eat it, and the whole food chain works.

But the warm waters that move east during the El Niño keep the cold water trapped in the deep ocean. The algae can't rise to the surface; fish die, fishermen are out of work, and there are no fish in the market.

The effects don't stop there. The warm ocean waters heat up the atmosphere and create thunderstorms that flood the South American coasts. The warm waters also build up a high-pressure area at the equator. As a result, unusual high- and low-pressure zones spring up above and below the equator, in the latitudes where most of the earth's population lives.

High- and low-pressure zones in the atmosphere are composed of different levels of temperature and humidity. They determine whether it will be cool and dry, or warm and rainy, or cold and snowy, or hot and dry. Pressure zones also affect the path of the high winds, called the jet stream, that blow in the upper level of the atmosphere, about nine miles (fifteen kilometers) above sea level. Jet stream winds are very strong, about 65 miles per hour (108 kilometers per hour).

This unusual pattern of pressure zones creates unusual weather. During the El Niño year, the winds high up in the jet stream become stronger. In an El Niño year, hurricanes that come barreling out of Africa toward Florida every summer and autumn clash with the jet stream winds. These reduce the power contained in the hurricanes' clouds, and the huge storms fizzle out in the mid-Atlantic.

Scientists now can see that the El Niño affects weather not only in North and South America, but in Australia and Africa as well. In the same way that farmers used to predict the severity of a winter by judging the fuzziness of caterpillar coats, climatologists

In these pictures of the earth from space, the clouds that cling to the equator develop over the region where the ocean flowing from the northern hemisphere meets the ocean flowing from the southern hemisphere. Exactly where the clouds form (above or below the equator) is determined by the strength of the wind. Strong winds blowing from the north, for example, can send the clouds south. For farmers and people who depend on annual monsoons, or rainy periods, as in India and Africa, these clouds are very important. Credit: NASA Headquarters, Earth Sciences and Applications Division.

can say with some confidence that during El Niño years, it will rain more in California and be dry in Australia and East Africa.

la niña

El Niño has an accomplice: a little sister named La Niña, which seems to follow on the heels of El Niño.

During a La Niña, the events of El Niño are reversed: the trade winds moving toward the equator are powerful and the equatorial ocean current is strong enough to move the warm Pacific waters to the west. Meanwhile, moving up the South American coast is the deep cold current that was kept down during the El Niño. It wells to the surface and brings up lots of algae, which feeds phytoplankton, which feed zooplankton, which feed fish, which put the fishermen back in business.

But when the cold waters meet the warm waters off Hawaii, the two extremes create thunderstorms. These create other unusual high- and low-pressure zones over North America.

During the La Niña, the jet stream is pushed north, and spring rains usually intended for Iowa fall in Alberta, Canada. High-pressure zones lock this system in place, and rains just don't fall where people expect them. When rains are locked out of a particular area for a whole season, a drought will result.

Scientists were happy to have discovered at least one cause of the 1988–1989 drought in the American Midwest.

But neither the El Niño nor the La Niña explain another climate change—the rise in global temperatures.

and the real culprit is . . .

For a while scientists split into three groups: those who believed the earth would heat up enough to cause the ice at the poles to melt, causing droughts everywhere and some places, like New York City, to be underwater; and those who believed we were on the verge of a new ice age, which comes in ten thousand-year cycles, during which the air cools, and the snow that falls in the winter just doesn't melt in the summer; and those who believed that both might happen: Whatever is causing the earth to heat up will cancel out any new ice age.

One of the first questions climatologists ask is: Has this all happened before?

The earth thrives on movement and change. Every 100,000 years or so, the shape of the earth's orbit around the sun changes from circular to elliptical.

In its orbit, the earth spins like a top, and the axis on which it spins returns to the same point every 21,000 years. Because the spin is slowing down, it has an occasional wobble.

The angle of the tilt of the earth's axis also changes every 40,000 years.

Both of these movements affect weather.

So do sunspots, which occur every eleven years and send out solar winds that heat up the earth.

So does the moon. Every month its orbit around the Earth affects ocean tides. And the moon returns to the same point in its revolution around the earth every nineteen or so years.

The interchange of movement might not stop with our own solar system. What effects do the movements of our galaxy, or of the most distant quark in the universe, have on the earth's weather?

But back to the crime lab.

out of the dark and distant past

To find clues from the past, scientists called dendrochronologists studied ancient tree rings, which are sensitive recorders of climate change. Tree rings also give fairly accurate dates, as long as you know the date of the tree ring you start counting with.

They revealed a very warm period all over the globe from 1100 to 1375 (a time of the Crusades in Europe, kingly empires in Africa, and mesa cities built by Anasazi in the American Southwest). That period equals about nine generations, or the time from your great-great-great-great-great-grandparents to you—a long time to be warm. Tree rings also revealed a very cold period (icy rivers in California, snow in June in New York) from 1450 to 1850, or thirteen generations.

So one clue that we are living at a point of climate change is that our grandparents remember hearing from their grandparents about different weather than we experience today.

But the record of the past goes way back and reveals other cycles, some of which may overlap.

into the archives

Cores drilled out of a rock formation in an ancient lake bed in New Jersey confirmed enormous climate cycles that coincided with changes in the shape of the earth's orbit 100,000 and 400,000 years ago. Rock cores also revealed a 40,000-year cycle change brought about by the interactions of the orbits of the earth and the moon. From the same rock, the scientists believe they have evidence of a climate cycle that repeats every two *million* years.

Nor did they stop there.

Ice cores from glaciers in Greenland and the Antarctic that

froze and trapped dust particles from tens of thousands of years ago yield clues that fires once raged across ancient forests, which were triggered by droughts caused by the El Niño–La Niña ocean pattern.

Scientists in the Ocean Drilling Program drilled into sediment under the ocean and brought up untouched layers of deep sea sediment full of clues from 600 feet below the ocean floor off Santa Barbara, California. Deep-ocean data from 150,000 years ago show that ice once covered the California coast. The cores also revealed that the sea level was 400 feet lower 18,000 years ago than it is today.

meanwhile, in space

Trying to figure out which cycle our climate might be in, or if it is part of one or two or more cycles, scientists take to the skies. While you sleep and when you are awake, in summer, winter, spring, and fall, hundreds of satellites continuously survey the earth, snapping pictures—some at the same point on the earth every revolution; others, every few square kilometers; and others, one continuous picture. Some satellites are sponsored by NASA (National Aeronautics and Space Administration), NOAA (National Oceanic and Atmospheric Administration), and NCAR (the National Center for Atmospheric Research); others are joint projects involving many countries.

If a person could ride as a photographer on a satellite and snap pictures of the ocean from space, he or she would follow the flow of the deep blue salty ocean currents in their graceful swim around the earth. One current in the North Atlantic circles Green-

This is a night launch of a weather balloon that will gather data on temperature, humidity, and wind conditions that might predict storms. National Center for Atmospheric Research/ University Corporation for Atmospheric Research/ National Science Foundation.

land and heads for Norway before going south to the Antarctic. Then the warm, lighter-green Gulf Stream clings to the North American coast on its autumn trip north toward Newfoundland. These currents affect weather in the atmosphere. Some weather will cause droughts.

A photographer sees surface wind eddies over the ocean, while altimeters in the spacecraft (if it were the *Topex-Poseidon,* for example) calculate wave height. Wave height is believed to influence humidity in the atmosphere, and winds influence what type of cloud will form. Changes in ocean color show the movement of vast areas of phytoplankton, and whether it is living or dead. If it's a La Niña year, there will be vast seas of phytoplankton off South America.

The glare from the ice over the poles reflecting sunlight and heat back into space is so bright a photographer needs sunglasses to look at it. The glare, called the *albedo,* is also blinding over deserts and big clouds. The temperature of the earth is affected by the amount of heat reflected back into space.

Clouds' shape and size indicate heat and humidity over the ocean. Besides being transporters of weather, clouds contain dust particles, or aerosols, blown up from volcanoes and deserts, as well as from fires set by people. Aerosols are clues that will tell how much humans influence weather.

hotter and hotter?

The temperature of the earth is rising, and it's the atmospheric heat that has most scientists puzzled and worried.

Most of the sun's rays directed at the earth are dangerous for life. We can see evidence of too much sun in deserts and drought areas: life needs water and the proper balance of oxygen and carbon dioxide to live. In fact, the first life on earth came out of the ocean. Green algae makes food with the help of the sun in the process called photosynthesis. They breathe in CO_2 and exhale oxygen which, with nitrogen, is what makes life possible.

Surrounding the earth in a protective embrace is an invisible atmosphere. In the stratosphere, between 20 and 80 miles (30 and 128 kilometers) above the earth is a band of ozone, a form of oxygen. The ozone layer blocks out the sun's ultraviolet rays, which

ATMOSPHERE

TROPOSPHERE

Where clouds form and weather develops. Controls the temperature of the earth. Greenhouse gases collect here. Most jet airplanes fly around 35,000 thousand feet. *Tropos* is a Greek word that means to turn or to change.

STRATOSPHERE

Supersonic jets fly in the lower levels of the stratosphere. The ozone layer, a band of oxygen (O_3), filters out rays from the sun that are harmful to life on Earth. *Stratus* is a Latin word that means covering.

MESOPHERE

This level is cold and dry and has huge windstorms. It is from the Greek word, *mesos,* meaning middle.

THERMOSPHERE

The temperature actually rises at the top of the thermosphere to 32° F. But life would perish here because there is no protection from the sun. It is from the Greek word, *thermos,* meaning heat.

are harmful to life on earth. The holes in the ozone layers over the Antarctic and the Arctic and the general thinning of the ozone layer everywhere have probably been caused by manmade chemicals. Scientists have discovered that this loss of ozone has been caused by a buildup of freon and chlorofluorocarbons, gases used in the manufacture of air conditioners and in aerosol spray cans. A worldwide ban on these chemicals, it is hoped, will stop some of the damage to the ozone layer.

The earth reflects right back some of the sun's radiation from the polar ice caps and deserts. In other areas, the sun's heat is stored in the ocean and land, then sent back into the atmosphere as infrared rays. Some infrared rays go back into space, but most join up with water vapor and the gases that form the layer of the atmosphere known as the greenhouse band: carbon dioxide, methane, chlorofluorocarbons, and nitrous oxide.

The trick is the balance.

This greenhouse band controls the temperature of the earth. If there were too little of the CO_2 and other gases in the atmosphere, the earth would freeze like Mars. If there was too much, the earth would fry like Venus. The levels of gases in the greenhouse band have risen, trapping more of the infrared heat that would normally go into space. This is causing a rise in the temperature of the atmosphere, and a rise in the temperature of the earth.

Scientists believe some of the increase in greenhouse gases is the result of humans burning coal and oil, or what are called fossil fuels, in cars and industrial manufacturing. (Long ago the fuels were living organisms that got buried in the rock sediments of the old earth. Because they were once alive, they give off carbon dioxide when they are burned.)

Another cause is the cutting down and burning of trees. Trees breathe in CO_2 and give off oxygen. When whole rain forests are burned, not only do the burning trees give off CO_2, but so does the rotting humus on the forest floor that becomes exposed.

Other causes might be natural and part of some long-term cycles that control the earth's weather. During a La Niña, for example, the dead algae that have fallen to the cold ocean bottom rise to the surface and release CO_2 into the atmosphere.

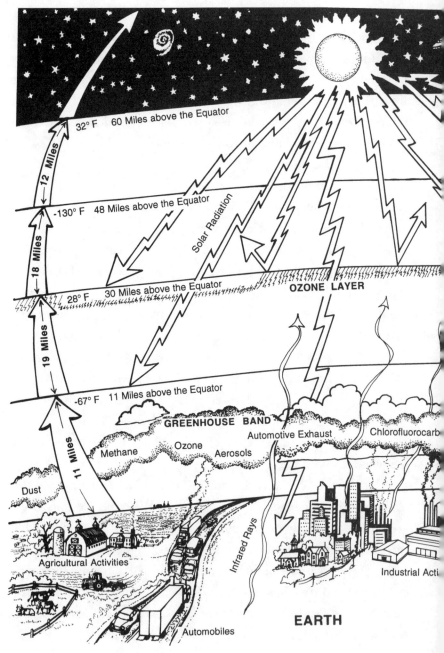

32° F   60 Miles above the Equator

12 Miles

-130° F   48 Miles above the Equator

18 Miles

Solar Radiation

28° F   30 Miles above the Equator   **OZONE LAYER**

19 Miles

-67° F   11 Miles above the Equator

GREENHOUSE BAND

Automotive Exhaust   Chlorofluorocarb

Methane   Ozone   Aerosols

11 Miles

Dust

Infrared Rays

Agricultural Activities

Industrial Acti

Automobiles   **EARTH**

N. J. Wylie.

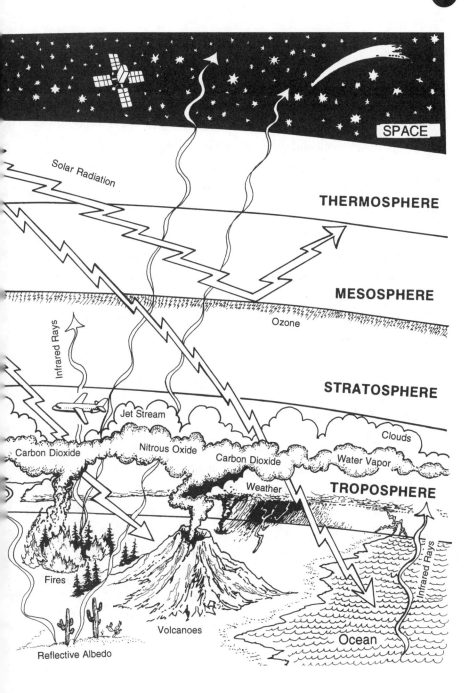

Some scientists claim that cattle and other grazing animals give off a lot of methane from their digestive systems. Scientists studying termites claim that termites produce more methane in a year than all industrial activity. Termites excrete a methane-containing substance when they build their mounds.

Erupting volcanoes give off CO_2.

Maybe it's all part of a natural cycle.

Maybe it's partly a natural cycle and partly the effects of man's activities.

Whatever the cause, the increase in the levels of CO_2 and methane in the greenhouse band means that earth's temperature will continue to rise. Rising temperatures will affect weather, and weather systems will change. Scientists predict that it will rain more in some places and less in others. This means that some places that are usually filled with lakes and ponds will experience drought. It also means that droughts may become more severe.

so who did it?

The culprit(s) of climate change are still at large, hiding out someplace where the eyes in the sky cannot see them, or buried within some mountains of computer readouts.

Now that we know more about the earth's weather, we know if it rains on our picnic, the rain might be caused by the earth's entering a cycle of influence with the orbit of the moon, and not just by a storm that came out of nowhere. The earth is truly a cosmic unit.

Rainmakers

The idea of coaxing nature to make rain has been around for a long time. Techniques vary from performing certain tribal dances, as done by Native Americans and other cultures around the world, to sending silver iodide particles into clouds using small devices fired from airplane wings.

The problem is that no technique always works, but each works often enough to make the technicians try to perfect their methods.

The nineteenth century was a time not only of great droughts in the central and western United States, but of wild scientific experiments. Ideas grew like weeds, and scientists able to collect enough money for homegrown projects were usually able to enlist enough friends to test them.

One of the earliest theories developed by Native Americans was that rising columns of heat created rainclouds. People lit fires

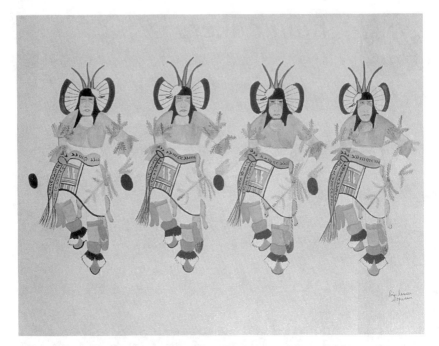

Rain dances are performed each year before planting by many Native American tribes. Dancers wear bright costumes and sing and dance to the rhythm of drums to please the gods to bring rain to the new crops. This dance, in 1960, was depicted in a watercolor painting by Encarnaçion Peña in San Ildefonso, New Mexico. Photo Archives, National Museum of the American Indian, Smithsonian Institution.

on hilltops to attract rain to their fields. Using this technique, rainmaker James Espy envisioned providing rain for the entire country. His scheme, to create forty-acre forest fires twenty miles apart once a week, fortunately was never tested.

Another popular theory was that noise attracted rain. This idea came from soldiers having witnessed rainstorms after battles during the Civil War. In ancient Greece two thousand years before, Plutarch had also noticed that it seemed to rain after noisy battles.

So in the early 1900s, rainmaker Robert Dyrenforth set off

barrages of field artillery outside San Antonio, Texas, during November and December. No rain resulted, but he made a lot of noise, and a lot of citizens were angry enough to complain.

In California, rainmaker Charles Hatfield did enough right for a few years to be employed by farmers in the San Joaquin Valley, who paid him between five hundred and a thousand dollars per

Rainmaker Charles Hatfield mixes his chemicals before burning them on top of a wood tower. His chemicals remain a mystery, but Hatfield was successful in bringing rain to California in the early 1900s.
Security Pacific National Bank Photograph Collection/Los Angeles Public Library.

inch of rain. Hatfield built twenty-foot wood towers, at the top of which he mixed secret chemicals whose reactions set off precipitation in clouds. But his success was a two-edged sword. He also was blamed for a serious flood in San Diego and was driven out of California and the rainmaking business by lawsuits. No one knows what his secret chemicals were.

Lawsuits also caused a prosperous rainmaker in Massachusetts to close up shop. Wallace Howell was hired by the city of New York to do something about a year-long drought, from 1949 to 1950, which had reduced the city's reservoirs by two-thirds. New Yorkers cut back on showers, dishwashing, and car washes; restaurants no longer served water with meals; and at least one teacher cut out water colors in her art classes. The water commissioner asked men not to shave on Fridays and to wear their beards as "a badge of honor."

Howell and his associates used a plane to inject dry ice (solid carbon dioxide) into clouds expected to pass over New York City. But from April to November in 1950, it barely rained at all. Then in December, it poured, and the drought ended in a rainfall that caused extensive flooding. Angry businessmen sued the city for two million dollars, claiming that the rainmaker the city had hired had caused the damage. Howell had no choice but to deny the flooding was from his rainmaking activities, so he could not take credit for having caused the rain, either.

silver iodide

In the late 1940s a General Electric researcher named Bernard Vonnegut devised a system for seeding clouds without having to use a plane. Working with an earlier idea that dry ice created ice crystals in clouds, he perfected a method of vaporizing silver iodide to produce crystals. Silver iodide has a molecular structure like that of ice crystals.

In generators on the ground the crystals were heated into a vapor that rose on a column of heated air into clouds, where the silver iodide bonded onto water droplets and caused it to rain.

"Cloud seeding does the same thing that nature does," says meteorologist Thomas Henderson of Atmospherics, Inc., a weather modification company in Fresno, California. "Because of that, it's hard to say which part is our part, and which part is nature's." A long-term study in one target area indicated that cloud seeding increased by 10 to 15 percent the amount of rain or snow that might otherwise have fallen.

Radar system used as field headquarters for Atmospherics, Inc., rainmaking company. The system tracks the storms through the area and provides information on clouds which can be used to direct seeding. Atmospherics, Incorporated.

Pyrotechnic seeding devices attached to the aircraft are ignited from control box inside the cabin. Units burn in place and provide the silver iodide nuclei. Atmospherics, Incorporated.

Getting the silver iodide crystals into the right cloud at the right time in the right place is not easy. "We have better instruments now, and radar and computers tell us when, where, and inside which cloud," says Henderson. "But nature does curious things all the time, and it might naturally produce something unusual during the time of seeding."

Pilots are on call at Atmospherics, Inc. for the Southern California Edison Company's cloud seeding project anytime storm clouds head into the San Joaquin Valley. They try to add to the amount of rain that falls during the winter months and to increase the amount of snow that falls in mountains of the Sierra Range.

They fly planes with pyrotechnic seeding devices, something like fireworks rockets, on the trailing edges of their wings. Inside the devices, silver iodide is heated and released as a smoke that contains microscopic particles of silver iodide, which measure .1 to .01 microns in diameter, a lot smaller than the periods on this page. Each gram of silver iodide in a pyrotechnic device produces about 1,000,000,000,000,000 (one quadrillion) tiny crystals, which act as the kernels, or nuclei, around which the ice forms in clouds.

These crystals bond with the droplets of moisture inside the cloud and freeze them into ice crystals. It takes one million to five million cloud droplets to make one raindrop.

The type of cloud determines where the plane will release the particles. Sometimes the plane flies directly through the cloud and seeds it; or it releases the silver iodide particles near the top of the cloud. If the cloud is a cumulus, with lots of updraft, the plane

Silver iodide artificial ice nuclei can be generated from units positioned at strategic locations on the ground, like this remote-control installation in the Sierra Nevada Mountain Range in California. Atmospherics, Incorporated.

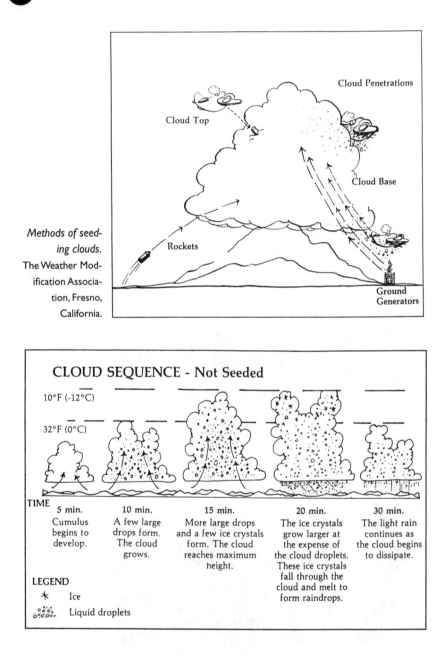

Methods of seed-
ing clouds.
The Weather Mod-
ification Associa-
tion, Fresno,
California.

Cloud Penetrations

Cloud Top

Cloud Base

Rockets

Ground
Generators

CLOUD SEQUENCE - Not Seeded

10°F (-12°C)

32°F (0°C)

TIME

5 min.	10 min.	15 min.	20 min.	30 min.
Cumulus begins to develop.	A few large drops form. The cloud grows.	More large drops and a few ice crystals form. The cloud reaches maximum height.	The ice crystals grow larger at the expense of the cloud droplets. These ice crystals fall through the cloud and melt to form raindrops.	The light rain continues as the cloud begins to dissipate.

LEGEND

✱   Ice

°₀°₀° Liquid droplets

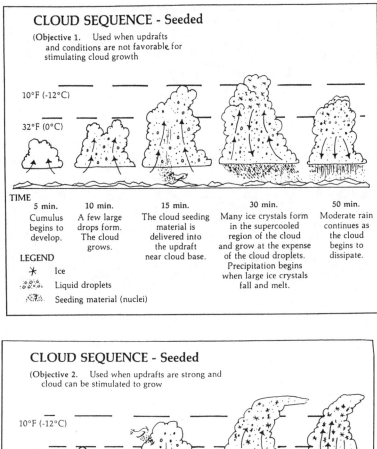

CLOUD SEQUENCE - Seeded
(Objective 1.   Used when updrafts
and conditions are not favorable for
stimulating cloud growth

10°F (-12°C)

32°F (0°C)

TIME

5 min.	10 min.	15 min.	30 min.	50 min.
Cumulus begins to develop.	A few large drops form. The cloud grows.	The cloud seeding material is delivered into the updraft near cloud base.	Many ice crystals form in the supercooled region of the cloud and grow at the expense of the cloud droplets. Precipitation begins when large ice crystals fall and melt.	Moderate rain continues as the cloud begins to dissipate.

LEGEND

✳ Ice

°⊙°⊙° Liquid droplets

⠐⣿⠄ Seeding material (nuclei)

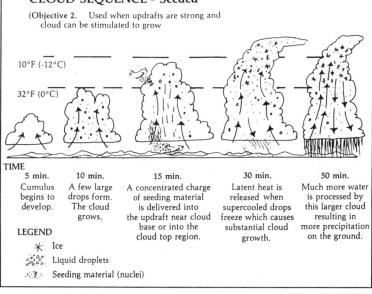

CLOUD SEQUENCE - Seeded
(Objective 2.   Used when updrafts are strong and
cloud can be stimulated to grow

10°F (-12°C)

32°F (0°C)

TIME

5 min.	10 min.	15 min.	30 min.	50 min.
Cumulus begins to develop.	A few large drops form. The cloud grows.	A concentrated charge of seeding material is delivered into the updraft near cloud base or into the cloud top region.	Latent heat is released when supercooled drops freeze which causes substantial cloud growth.	Much more water is processed by this larger cloud resulting in more precipitation on the ground.

LEGEND

✳ Ice

°⊙°⊙° Liquid droplets

⠄⣿⠄ Seeding material (nuclei)

Seeded portion (center) of cloud line shows conversion of droplets to ice crystals and light rain falling. Nonseeded portions, right and left, show no ice crystals. Atmospherics Incorporated.

will release the particles at the base of the cloud. Electrical signals from cockpit computers indicate when to dispense the vaporized silver iodide particles.

On the ground, generators placed close to clouds at altitudes of four thousand to five thousand feet in the Sierra Mountains heat the silver iodide solution to 1,560 degrees Fahrenheit (850 degrees Celsius). The silver and iodide in the vapor then recombine to form tiny crystals of silver iodide, which are released into passing clouds.

Once the cloud is seeded, it's in the hands of the winds. That means that the rain that is badly needed in a drought area can fall across the boundary in another state, perhaps even in a river that is about to flood. Sometimes when the air temperature is very hot, the rain evaporates before it reaches the ground. In very severe droughts, there may be no clouds at all to be seeded. Or it might not rain at all, and farmers who have hired rainmakers want their money back. You can see some of the legal, political, and economic problems involved in cloud seeding.

Rainmakers are a little like magicians, and if their tricks fail, they are laughed off the stage. But as long as there is drought, there will be a demand for them.

Drought on an Island: Antigua

Antigua rose out of the Caribbean Sea in a violent explosion 34 million years ago, the product of an undersea volcano. When its lava cooled, volcanic ash developed into the rich clay soil that made the island into a tropical rain forest.

As recently as four hundred years ago, if you had been shipwrecked on one of its sandy beaches, you would have crawled onto a paradise island. Seabirds would have announced your arrival in the dense jungle where parrots squawked and big-winged butterflies flew among perfumed flowers and trees with leaves large enough to build a shelter. You would have eaten well: trees were filled with clusters of yellow bananas and heavy orange mangoes, small animals raced through the underbrush, and the clear sea teemed with fish and shellfish. You would have collected more than enough rainwater to drink and bathe in. Nor would you have been alone. Arawak Indians called the island home, as did an occasional pirate who hid his ship and buried his treasure (it's rumored) in one of the small coves and inlets.

One of the islands in the Antilles chain that ring the Caribbean Sea, Antigua is not very big—180 square miles (280 square kilometers), and almost round. On the shores of the warm, blue sea, resort hotels open their doors to tourists who come from around the world. Soft winds caress the 365 white sand beaches ("one for every day of the year," travel brochures say), where you can swim and snorkle, windsurf, sail, and scuba dive. Except for a few villages in the center of the island, most Antiguans live near St. John's, the city on the northwest side, which has a population of about thirty thousand. "It's so crowded," said an Antiguan, "that when you get up, you can open the shutters in your house and shake hands with your neighbor in his house."

But the rain forest is a thing of the past. Christopher Columbus landed on the island in 1493 and claimed the island for Spain, naming it Santa Maria de la Antigua, but in 1650, traders from Great Britain took it over. A couple of years later, they planted sugarcane as a cash crop. The British said later that the Spanish did not want Antigua because the climate was too dry.

As planters cut away the rain forest, fields of sugarcane gradually replaced the tropical jungle, and Antigua became a practically bald island. The planters did not think about the fact that they were causing long-term environmental damage. But ever since sugarcane replaced trees, Antigua's natural droughts have become extreme droughts.

Tourists don't know that Antigua suffers from serious drought. If you are there on holiday, you can take a shower anytime of day or swim in the clear, emerald-blue water of the hotel pool. But the 85,000 people who live there year round know it. A

Tourists see pictures like this one and think of tropical islands as being places with lots of water.

good day, they say, is one of the three days out of seven when they can turn on the tap and get water.

sugarcane plantation ghosts

The story starts about three hundred years ago.

Away from the beach, the island is a different world. Here, roads follow rolling hills dotted with herds of grazing goats and an occasional palm tree, past a few villages and some farms where one or two men or women bend over to break the soil with short-handled hoes. It's as if Antigua has two personalities: the one on the coast that travel brochures sell, and its quiet heart.

Two hundred years ago, today's abandoned plantations were thriving sugarcane industry production centers. Here thousands of slaves from West Africa worked in the tall, rustling cane fields, planting, cutting, and lifting under the hot sun, or in stormy rains, chanting rhythmic folksongs such as:

> *To fork the land*
> *We work,*
> *To cut the cane*
> *We work,*
> *To dig the root*
> *We work.*

In the spring, groups of children worked in "Little Gangs" and helped plant the cane by dropping dung into the holes for fertilizer. Norris Gregory, whose mother had ten children and worked on a plantation, was a member of a Little Gang when he was in elementary school. Now in his nineties and a retired carpen-

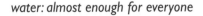

*Slaves form a line to work the land to plant sugarcane in Antigua. Illustrated London News,
June 9, 1849.*

ter, Gregory remembers hundreds of kids in the Little Gangs running through the fields to pick up the sharp remnants of cane after
the harvest.

Every day from dawn until late afternoon, men and women
hauled the cane into the stone windmill, where workers ground up
the stalks and put them into huge vats over fires that boiled the mass
into syrup. To make it into sugar, some of it was left to crystallize in
the sun. An acre of cane produced about a ton of sugar, and that
brought a lot of money at the market in Europe or America.

By 1750 most of Antigua's trees had been cut down to provide fields for sugarcane. Owned by British landowners who stayed

in England, the cane was strictly a private cash crop. (A cash crop is a farm product raised for cash from sales.) English managers, who oversaw the cane production, lived in the plantation houses. To them, life was good.

Slaves lived in crowded shacks on the plantations and grew their own food in small gardens. Life was not good. They were overworked and punished if they tried to flee. A rocky ledge on the east coast of the island is named Devil's Bridge. So many despairing slaves threw themselves off the ledge into the rough sea that people said the devil himself must live here.

After slavery was legally abolished in 1834, Antiguan workers named one of their towns *Liberta*—liberty. But they still worked in the cane fields for the same owners, the difference being that now they received a small wage. But with their wage they had

Workers inside an Antiguan sugar mill grind the cane. Illustrated London News, June 9, 1849.

to build their own shacks and buy their own food. They were not any better off.

water for the master, water for the slaves

Water was always a problem. During drought, plantation managers would allow workers to use their cattle ponds. Gregory remembers walking three or four miles a day to get water. "If you had a donkey, you carried an oil can on each side. If you didn't have a donkey, you just carried a pan on your head. That means you'd have to go back two or three times a day."

Samuel Smith, an Antiguan who lived to be 105, told his story to his grandchildren, Keithlyn and Fernando Smith, in a book titled *To Shoot Hard Labour.*

> The planters usually would use the drought as an excuse to cut the wages [he wrote]. Food was always hard to come by, but the situation would be severely worsened by the drought, so hunger and starvation were more common then. . . . The planters began to let the workers use the estate pond water . . . but the pond water was very unclean because plenty of crapaud [frogs] were living in them. . . . You see, animals too usually pass their urine and waste . . . and that kind of water was dangerous for health. . . . But we gladly drank that water, though. . . . It's like this: a crapaud and animal waste water, but man uses it and survives.

Drought and poor markets finally brought the sugarcane industry to a close about 1940. By that time, most Antiguans belonged to labor unions and had developed skills, such as carpentry, that took them off the plantations. Today, very few Antiguans have any desire to work as farmers. Most work in the tourist industry. "Everything from the past represents the negative," an Antiguan said. And so Antigua imports about 80 percent of its food.

bring back the trees

Even if Antiguans wanted to be farmers, the land still suffers. The soil was overworked during the continuous sugarcane production. But most important, to plant the land, sugarcane farmers cut down trees. And lack of trees contributes to drought.

Trees absorb carbon dioxide and give off oxygen and water vapor, which is why cool forests smell so fresh. Besides attracting rain, trees keep the land in place because their roots anchor the soil. They shade ponds and reservoirs, including the big reservoir, Potswork, built to hold water that is piped into houses. The average temperature in the summer in Antigua is more than 84 degrees Fahrenheit (29 degrees Celsius). The hot sun sucks up all water that is not in shade.

After the sugarcane fields were abandoned, the bare ground was exposed. The topsoil dried up and blew away in the constant trade winds. The blown-away topsoil settled underwater on the reef, smothering some coral and fish.

What sugarcane growing hasn't destroyed, grazing animals have. Goats and sheep and cattle, which graze anywhere in Antigua, eat the ground cover scrub that holds the soil in place.

Antigua: Goats and sheep graze everywhere in Antigua. They contribute to desertification.

Because the areas of greatest rain runoff near the reservoirs and ponds, called watershed areas, are not fenced, goats eat away the ground cover there, too.

Without topsoil, the exposed ground is hardened by the sun. Then when it rains, the rain just runs off the surface into puddles that evaporate, or back into the ocean. Rain doesn't penetrate the ground to seep into the aquifers. And the rain that runs into the reservoir and smaller ponds carries silt with it, so the reservoir water has to be filtered before it can be pumped through pipes. That drives up the water's price for the user.

Mangrove trees on the coasts trap some of the topsoil to

keep it from destroying the coral reef. Mangroves also keep out the saltwater that rushes into the aquifers after big storms. But when hotel developers bulldoze mangrove swamps to build hotels, salt-water penetrates the aquifers, and the coral reef is smothered with topsoil.

the drought of 1983–1984

Samuel Smith said he couldn't decide which caused more agony, hurricanes or drought, but thought drought did, because hurri-canes come and go, and you build up again, but you can't see a drought until it's on you and it brings painful hunger and disease.

Antigua has had many hurricanes but more devastating droughts, the first recorded in 1731. Others lasted for more than a year: 1871–1874, 1910–1912, and more recently, 1983–1984.

hauling water by barge

The El Niño was in effect in 1982–1983, and it rained only 22 inches (56 centimeters) in Antigua in 1983–1984, about half the average rainfall of 42 to 44 inches (107 to 112 centimeters). Antigua's one big reservoir, Potswork, dried up, and when all the smaller ponds dried up too, the government had to do something. So they contracted with the neighboring islands of Dominica and Guadaloupe to haul in about thirty million gallons of freshwater by barge.

When the barge docked in St. John's Harbor, the U.S. Navy carried it in trucks to station points throughout the island. Antiguans lined up with containers for their allotment. Because that took too long, the Navy placed World War II rubber rafts in villages and filled them with water so the villagers would have a

	HURRICANE	DROUGHT	EARTHQUAKE
1681	Severe		
1789			
1843			Severe
1847	Major sugar crop damage		
1871	Severe		
1871—1874		So severe many people migrated to other islands.	
1910—1912		So severe ponds and reservoirs were completely dry.	
1924	Severe: two in one season.		
1928	Severe		
1983—1984		So severe water was hauled by barge from other islands.	
1989	Severe		

In addition to its devastating droughts, Antigua is subject to frequent hurricanes and earth tremors. Antiguans experienced a severe earthquake in 1843.

constant supply. But the goats and sheep that roam free drank the same water. Some babies got severe diarrhea.

Pets and gardens died. Cows died, their bones draped with skin; and there was no milk. "Even the palm trees died," an Antiguan remembered, "and we would see dark clouds coming, but they were filled with dust, not rain."

the "desal"

After the severe drought in 1984, the government of Antigua contracted with a Japanese firm to build a desalination plant. Making saltwater into freshwater seemed to be the only option. But it was expensive.

Built from an Israeli design, the huge steam distillation plant cost between $50 and $75 million. It works in the same way—boiling and refining—that sugarcane is made into corn syrup.

What happens in the plant is simple: the cold seawater is piped into big cylinders. It is heated until it boils, which separates the brine from the water and produces a lot of steam. The steam rises and hits the cold seawater pipes and condenses into freshwater, which is captured. The salt and other minerals that fall to the bottom are piped back into the ocean. Then chemicals are added to cut down on bacteria and improve the taste, and freshwater is pumped out along pipes into reservoirs.

The trouble is Antigua needs about 3.5 million gallons of water a day. The desal plant provides only 2 million gallons a day. Full reservoirs can pump 1.8 million gallons a day, and wells and smaller ponds can provide about 1.2 million gallons a day, which, with the Desal, makes 5 million gallons. But during drought when the reservoirs are empty, the Desal can pump only about half the water that is needed.

On paper, the Desal is an ideal solution. But few technicians so far have been trained to maintain the system, and if it breaks down, it takes a long time to repair.

Meanwhile, Potswork reservoir is filled with silt from blown-away topsoil. Why not clean out the reservoir so that it can hold more water? It takes money and labor to do it, but Norris

STEAM DESALINATION

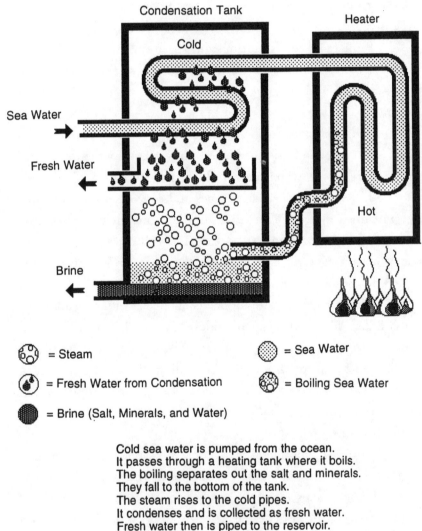

Condensation Tank
Heater
Cold
Sea Water
Fresh Water
Hot
Brine

(o) = Steam   (o) = Sea Water

(●) = Fresh Water from Condensation   (o) = Boiling Sea Water

● = Brine (Salt, Minerals, and Water)

Cold sea water is pumped from the ocean.
It passes through a heating tank where it boils.
The boiling separates out the salt and minerals.
They fall to the bottom of the tank.
The steam rises to the cold pipes.
It condenses and is collected as fresh water.
Fresh water then is piped to the reservoir.
The brine is piped back into the ocean.

Gregory remembers when the government hired "men and women, boys and girls" for a shilling a day to clean out the ponds. Now no one does it, even though Potswork was dry as a bone during the last drought.

Some of the water pipes are old and rusty. And often water doesn't even run through them. In St. John's, people say they get water three days a week if they are lucky. "Sometimes it comes on in the middle of the night when you're sleeping. It's not much more efficient than pan water or carrying it by donkey," Norris Gregory grumbles.

Many hotels have their own small desalination systems, but because tourism is the biggest industry, hotels are first on the list for piped water, too. About half the homes on Antigua have some kind of cistern, a big container that catches and stores rainwater or the Desal water when it does come through. "I have a catchment system, a low-flush toilet which I flush only when necessary, and I recycle my wastewater and put it on the plants." Veronica Michaels, of the Environmental Awareness Group in St John's, ticks off the ways in which she copes with the water problem. "But sometimes when it's terribly dry, I shoot the hose over the bare dirt in the front of the house to keep the dust down. I figure I have some water in the bank for that, although I feel bad about it."

environmental health

Some Antiguans see their island's environmental problems being as serious as a hurricane raging across the ocean.

Several international organizations have set up tree

nurseries. In an effort to replenish the tree population, gardeners plant thousands of seedlings that will one day fill the gaps left by the sugarcane industry.

Many kids are interested in Antigua's environment and belong to the Environmental Awareness Group in St. John's. They go on Saturday field trips to see problems firsthand. In a newsletter and on radio and TV spots, the group reminds all Antiguans to conserve water by not washing their cars and by turning off the faucet while they brush their teeth.

Lesroy Merchant lectures at an assembly at Princess Margaret High School in Antigua.

At the Princess Margaret High School, teacher Lesroy Merchant has set up a small garden that the students tend during and after school. He teaches correct irrigation, planting, and the pleasures of taking the vegetables to market and making money. "Farming is looked upon as having low wages and being dehumanizing," Merchant said. "This shows that agriculture can be worthwhile."

With proper management, someday Antigua could grow everything from nuts, mangoes, bananas, papayas, and pumpkins to sweet potatoes, beans, yams, and sea island cotton.

Merchant also formed the Cooperative Farmers Association, whose members—including teachers, lawyers, physicians, and managers—farm a few acres inland on an old plantation on weekends and after work, or after their daily swim.

One of the advantages of living in Antigua is being able to celebrate what they call "the life-giving sea." Sometimes in the early morning, sometimes during lunch hour, sometimes after work, Antiguans take time off for a swim. "In my younger days, I used to get up before dawn and walk nude to the beach from my house," remembers Norris Gregory. He still swims, but he goes to the beach later. "Now I have to wear clothes," he says.

no more ghosts

Antigua's problems are ghosts from the past.

"You cannot separate water from poverty in Antigua," says Merchant. The impoverished land was a legacy from a few who got rich a century ago. When water is scarce, the poor wait longer or walk farther for it.

Norris Gregory agrees. "I've lived with drought all my life," he said. "I hate injustice. I don't like advantaged people doing mean things to other people. When I am flying up to God, I want everything to be clear between him and me."

California: High-Tech Water

6

"Whiskey's for drinking, water's for fighting over."
Mark Twain, who was a journalist in San Francisco, said that a
hundred years ago about California. It is still true today.

California has lots of water. The problem is getting it
around the state so everyone has a fair share.

water lawyers

This is what Mark Twain meant. A hundred years ago, legislators
argued over how to get the water from the abundant runoff of the
Sierra Mountains in the north to the almost-desert in the south.
Then water lawyers argued over who had the rights to the water:
people who owned land on the banks of rivers and streams, or
those who had first discovered and used it. Now they argue over

how water should be distributed among farmers, city dwellers, and the environment.

Like divorcing parents arguing over their child's custody and failing to notice that their child has run away, water lawyers are surprised to discover that drought has put a whole new spin on the situation. In 1991, the seventh year of California's drought, the U.S. Congress passed a bill requiring farmers to sell some of their water to cities and to set aside about a million acre-feet of water for the environment. (An acre-foot is the amount of water that would cover one acre, about a football field, one foot deep; or 326,000 gallons, about the amount used by a family of four in two years.) "Water from *where?*" asks a farmer in the dusty San Joaquin Valley, where the annual allotment has been cut back by 50 percent. "If they can find it, they can have it."

ancient droughts

Drought is not new to California. Scientists reading ancient tree rings are able to identify periods of drought lasting from one to as many as forty years. The causes of these droughts are unknown, but the effect was the same then as now: it doesn't rain enough. In good years, storms full of precipitation blow in from the Pacific and sweep across northern California, leaving snow in the Sierras, which melts in the spring and pours into the hundreds of streams and rivers that fill the reservoirs and empty into the man-made canals that channel the water south. Some years it rains more than others.

CALIFORNIA RAIN AND SNOW

IT RAINS AND SNOWS AN
AVERAGE 193 MILLION
ACRE FEET EACH YEAR.

OF THAT, THE SUN DRINKS
AN AVERAGE 121 MILLION
ACRE FEET IN EVAPORATION
AND TRANSPIRATION.

OF THE 72 MILLION ACRE FEET LEFT,

32% GOES BACK TO THE OCEAN

31% GOES TO FARMING

29% GOES TO THE ENVIRONMENT

6% GOES TO CITIES AND INDUSTRY

2% RUNS OFF TO NEVADA

CALIFORNIA WATERWAYS

California waterways. Between the San Luis Reservoir, Mono Lake, and Los Angeles is the San Joaquin Valley. In the federal Central Valley Project there, 500 miles of canals transport 7.1 million acre-feet (AF) of water. Water from Shasta Lake in the north is funneled through miles of canals to water the San Joaquin Valley.

new droughts: cities

But the stress on the water system has come from a population explosion in the cities. There are more and more people who turn on their faucets not only to bathe and brush their teeth but also to water their lawns, wash their cars, and in some cases, fill their swimming pools. A study in southern California found that families with pools used an average of 54.7 extra gallons of water per day just to keep their pools full after evaporation and spillage.

Stress on water systems from cities has happened not just in California, but in Beijing, New Delhi, and other places around the world. The population of Los Angeles, for example—11.9 million people in 1992—is expected to jump to 13.2 million by the year 2000. The total population of California, 28 million in 1992, will increase to 36 million by 2010.

Fifty percent of all the people on the earth today live in cities; and specialists predict that by the turn of the century, that number will go up to 80 percent.

What will happen to farming? Will there be enough water for irrigation to provide food to feed all these people?

What will happen to the environment? Will there be enough wetlands for birds and rivers for fish?

These are some of the questions that California is facing at the moment.

gold and water

A hundred and fifty years ago, a prospector saw the jagged vein of gold in northern California that Spanish explorers had been seeking for years. Within two years, men from around the world left their jobs as clerks, fishermen, whalers, insurance salesmen, farmers, railroad workers, and road builders and went west. In one day they could find enough gold to equal what they would have earned in one year.

To feed the miners, ranchers raised cattle, and farmers planted hundreds of acres of wheat, which bakers worked overtime to make into bread to be loaded onto horse-drawn delivery carriages that raced into San Francisco before dawn.

Women, too, came by ship from the East and set up shops and opened libraries and staged evening concerts of classical music.

Gold ultimately made San Francisco into the gateway to the Far East, where trading ships docked, loaded with all kinds of exotic goods.

hydraulic mining

All of these refinements in San Francisco were support for the do-or-die, profit-seeking miners who spread out in the hills, competing fiercely to stake a claim to a particular area and to get the gold out of the hard-packed soil. The quickest way was to wash it out, using floppy sailcloth hoses. That required lots of water. So miners laid claim to streams and built dams to divert the water to their gold-filled hillside.

It wasn't long before a miner from Connecticut came up with the idea of the iron nozzle, which, attached to the cloth hose, could shoot water at a dazzling rate direct from the stream or river, up into the air and across hundreds of feet of land straight into the side of the mountain where it would wash away the dirt that covered the gold. Called the Little Giant, the hose with the nozzle shot water from an iron stand, resembled a cannon, and did about as much damage The new nozzles were so valuable that miners removed them at night, took them home to polish, and kept them under the bed while they slept.

As a result, tons of earth ran in mudslides down the hills, filled up rivers, and covered farmlands. Sand and gravel mixed with gold, called *slickens,* buried houses and ran in muddy streams

Iron nozzles attached to the ends of sailcloth hoses could direct water taken from rivers and streams and shoot it straight against a hillside to wash away the dirt that surrounded the vein of gold. These miners from Colorado about a century ago pose proudly with their iron nozzle. The Denver Public Library, Western History Department.

through towns, permanently anchoring unfortunate boats trapped in shallow streams.

The environment was the last thing miners had on their minds. It wasn't until 1884 that the government, seeing whole mountains washed away, outlawed hydraulic mining. But the damage had been done. The Little Giants had shot water straight up to the sun, had dried up wells, and drained whole tributaries. What land was left had no trees, no grass, no plants.

the first water laws

The fights over water began here, and two major laws that determine water rights in California grew out of this early use of water.

One is called prior appropriation; the other is riparian rights. The miners who had laid claim to the streams did so on the basis of I-saw-it-first-so-it's-mine. Later, water lawyers called this kind of water right *prior appropriation*—first in time, first in right.

Those who are lucky enough to own land on riverbanks have *riparian rights* (after the Latin *ripa,* for riverbank), and they can use the water for whatever they want.

But imagine that your house is on the bank of a stream, and you go out one morning and discover that it is almost dry. This is what happened over and over in California. Miners with prior appropriation rights a few miles upstream on the same stream built dams and diverted riparian owners' water.

Now imagine it the other way around: the riparian owner is upstream, and *he* diverts water being used downstream by a prior appropriator, who goes out one morning and finds the stream dry.

Water lawyers argued over who could legally use the water. The legislature decided in 1873 in a law called the California Doctrine that both could use the water *as long as it was for beneficial purposes, and as long as the users didn't pollute it.*

The law also said that prior appropriators had to use their water or lose it. (This became very important later.)

Q: *In California, who owns the water in a river?*

1. the riparian owner
2. the prior appropriator
3. the state

The state owns the water. But all can use it — as long as they understand the water laws.

making a paradise in the dry south

Seventy-five percent of California's water is in the north. But seventy-five percent of the state's need for water is in the south, where farmlands and cities have grown up out of the dry plains.

Los Angeles began as a market town near the ranches and farms that were begun to provide food for early settlers. Pictures from the early 1900s show horse-drawn water vendors selling water to residents, and huge waterwheels, like ferris wheels, scooping up water from streams and dumping it into collection tanks.

Today Los Angeles is one of the most important cities in the world. It owes its success not to the movie industry, not to Disneyland, but to the world's most sophisticated man-made water delivery system.

Hundreds of miles of interconnected dams, reservoirs, canals, and aqueducts, built by the state and the federal government for the past hundred years, evenly distribute water around

In 1876, a winemaker named Thomas Leahy built a waterwheel on his dry land in Los Angeles to provide water for his grapes. Today the dirt road is a major thoroughfare, and his waterwheel has been replaced with a skyscraper whose water comes from northern California, 500 miles away. Security Pacific National Bank Photograph Collection/Los Angeles Public Library.

the state. Even water from the mighty Colorado River, which waters seven states and Mexico, was diverted via a canal to bring water to parched southern California. An astronomer on Mars looking at the California water network would conclude that there definitely was intelligent life on Earth.

The California Aqueduct is 444 miles of straight canal. In 1992, water levels were dangerously low.

water to farms

California has been called the fruit and vegetable basket of the country because it provides so much market produce. But most of the goods raised for export are grown in one of the driest areas of all: the San Joaquin Valley.

Farmers who moved by the hundreds from the drought-stricken Midwest in the 1930s were so relieved to be in their new paradise, they ignored occasional droughts. They built wells and pumped up groundwater and collected rainfall.

To make settlement even more attractive, the federal Bureau of Reclamation created the Central Valley Project, which encouraged farmers to buy and settle on 160-acre farms adjacent to water in the canals that they had built. The price of the water was

kept very low—only a few dollars an acre-foot to encourage settlers. In 1982 that acreage limit was raised to 960 acres, still with
cheap water.

   Unfortunately—and here's where the water lawyers come

*The U.S. Bureau of Reclamation built several dams and reservoirs in the California water
distribution system as part of the Central Valley Project, designed to bring water to farmland.
This reservoir at Shasta Lake sends water south to the San Joaquin Valley. Snow-covered
Mount Shasta rises in the background. Its melted snow provides water for the lake.*
National Oceanic and Atmospheric Administration.

in—users of federally subsidized water in the Central Valley Project were considered to have prior appropriation rights, which meant they had to use it or lose it. The intention was that if farmer Brown, who had rights to four acre-feet of water, used only two acre-feet, he must give up the extra two acre-feet to someone who needed it.

However, since farmer Brown might not use four acre feet of water *this* year, but might need it *next* year, he had to do something with it to keep it. And he still had to conform to the laws that said he must use it for beneficial purposes and could not pollute it.

blame it on the cows

This is where the system got abused. To keep his water, he could grow water-sucking plants like alfalfa or rice. Or he could keep a herd of cattle, which would not only drink water but eat water-sucking plants like alfalfa. Rich ranchers and corporations bought up lots of land, and the cheap water rights with it. They dumped millions of acre-feet of unused water when they needed to keep their rights to it.

The luckiest farmers are the ones with riparian rights. They can divert their streams onto their land and use the water to irrigate their crops and for any other purpose. "A farmer would sell his wife before he sold his water rights," said a farmer in the San Joaquin Valley.

And so traditions that created the problems of today were set early in California:

- Laws that governed who could use the water and how it was used

- Cities and farms in arid plains
- Farmers growing things with cheap, federally subsidized water that they had to use or lose
- Lots of water wasted by big landowners
- Increased population
- Drought

Put this all together with people in cities who get fined for using too much water or who are not allowed to water their lawns or wash their cars, and you get people who begin to resent farmers using their cheap water to grow water-sucking plants like alfalfa and to raise herds of cattle only so they don't lose their water rights.

Eighty to eighty-five percent of all *developed* water (water that is held in reservoirs and fed through canals and aqueducts with metered delivery outlets) goes to farms. The problem is that the water is shooting through 1960s canals at 1930s prices, a fraction of what city dwellers pay for water.

Ask any Californian who is not a farmer who has the most water and he will answer, "Farmers! And they get it at a government-subsidized price!"

"What do they think I'm going to do? Sell my water to Saudi Arabia?" asks a small farmer in the San Joaquin Valley. He is talking about the new law requiring farmers to give up some of their water.

California grows nearly 100 percent of all the almonds, artichokes, dates, figs, kiwifruits, olives, pistachios, pomegranates, prunes, raisins, and walnuts grown in the United States, and half the national supply of other fruits and vegetables. Very few farmers raise cattle or grow alfalfa, but cattle products—beef, milk, cream, and cheese—rank first in California agricultural produce.

But when water lawyers begin arguing on behalf of cities or the environment, they argue like this:

- Farm produce overall constitutes only 9 to 10 percent of California's gross domestic product (GDP), yet uses 80 to 85 percent of the state's developed water, or 31 percent of California's annual supply of water.
- Industry and cities, where most of the population live and work, use only 2.1 percent of their developed water or 6 percent of the state's annual water supply.

Therefore, throw out the farmers, some lawyers argue.

the environment

Environmentalists agree, but for other reasons. They monitor California's distribution of water to wildlife.

The most dramatic event occurred in 1983 at the Kesterton National Wildlife Refuge, near the San Joaquin Valley. Scientists found not only a huge number of dead birds, but many with birth defects, such as one wing, three legs, and twisted heads. Whatever affected the birds did not smell or sting.

Searching for clues in what they called the Three Mile Island of Irrigated Farmland, scientists discovered a buildup of selenium, an element that occurs naturally in the soil and is harmless in small quantities, but toxic in large quantities. "birds don't know the water is poisoned," said an environmentalist. "They'll go wherever there is warm water." The cause of the selenium buildup: lack of proper distribution of drainage from farmlands.

Land naturally contains salts and minerals. Well-drained

land that gets lots of rain doesn't allow salts and minerals to build up. Sometimes there is a layer of clay soil beneath the topsoil that doesn't allow the water containing salts and minerals to drain rapidly. So the soil near the root zone becomes waterlogged, and the water is potentially poisonous. This also happens during drought years. When it rains a lot, concentrations of these poisons are diluted or washed away. Or farmers can install drainage pipes. Buried in the ground, these have holes in them, collect the excess water, and pipe it somewhere else.

But where do you put it?

This was the problem in Kesterton. The refuge was to be used for two purposes: as a wildlife refuge and as an irrigation dump. Selenium and other minerals and salts from farm irrigation collected in the refuge ponds and contaminated the water. Bugs and grubs ate the contaminated plankton in the water, birds ate the bugs and grubs, and the poisonous selenium spread throughout the whole system.

Gradually, scientists realized what was happening, and the refuge was closed.

Environmentalists also blamed the farmers.

are all farmers really guilty?

"If I am ever reincarnated, I hope it's as a California water lawyer," said Ted Sheely, a farmer in the San Joaquin Valley. "They'll never be poor."

Sheely has spent the morning calling his congressmen in Washington from the cellular phone in his trailer office, pleading with them to fight the new water bill that will force farmers to give up even more water to the environment and to cities. He doubts that the congressmen who will vote for the bill have his best interests at heart.

"Take my water, take my land. It's worth nothing to me without water," he says.

He slams the door to his 4-wheel drive and heads out across the straight, flat roads that intersect his one thousand acres. It's harvest time, and huge bales of cotton stand along the sides of the road waiting to be picked up to be taken to the cotton mill, visible on the distant flat horizon about five miles away.

"People say we're using all the water, but we're not using all the water. With drought, if anyone has an overall solution, I don't know what it is. I make little cuts here and there," Sheely says. "Then after a time, there's nothing more to cut."

Being a farmer means that he has to read the market before the seed is even in the ground. Crop price is negotiated and the crops are sold long before planting, then delivered at harvest. This year for the first time Sheely grew safflower. "I'll grow rubber trees if latex is in demand. Or I'll raise catfish in ponds. I don't care. I just have to service my debt until the drought is over, when I hope to make a profit again."

banks: the bottom line

After deciding what they will grow, farmers go to the bank for a loan to buy the necessary equipment to raise and harvest the crop. But with the drought in its seventh year, bankers think long and hard before they give loans to California farmers.

"The first thing they ask is what is your source of water. If you don't have one, you don't get a loan. A lot of little farmers are already out of business. My water comes from Mount Shasta,"

Sheely says, referring to the federal water that irrigates his crops. "But this year I've had to dig wells." Sheely gets 2.6 acre-feet from Mount Shasta, short of the ideal 3 acre-feet.

high-tech farms

Digging wells, Sheely says, is a short-term solution, because the water table drops. On his desk is a picture of his two-year-old son, with a wide smile on his face, wearing a hard hat and covered with dirt. "That's my helper," says Sheely.

One of the smaller canals in the San Joaquin Valley is almost completely dry in 1992.

Acres of dry soil and difficulty in getting water forced many small farmers to sell their farms during the worst California drought in modern times in the late 1980s and early 1990s.

To water his safflower, he dug a series of shallow, fifteen-foot wells, and set up a master panel of switches and buttons to control the pumping. One day he was lucky to find a deep, long-unused well, dug in 1948, that he is cleaning out with a vacuum powered by the diesel engine from his old truck. Last year Sheely experimented with a double-walled well. Its inventor theorized that the double wall would create a vacuum that would increase the upward flow of the water and cut down on pumping costs. They tapped water 2,100 feet down, but the ground above and around the well collapsed and crushed it.

After the bank grants a loan, Sheely has to judge if what he is doing is cost-effective, that is, justifies the initial cost.

"I ask, how much water can I afford to pump?" he says.

Ted Sheely and some of the irrigation pipes that carry water from the pump on the left. A switchboard allows him to start any of several pumps on his shallow wells.

Ted Sheely and an assistant start the diesel engine that pumps water from 2,250 feet down.

"At sixty-five dollars an acre-foot, I'm okay. But if it goes up to a hundred and fifty dollars, I can't afford it. You learn to be cautious. I learned this in the school of hard knocks. I didn't learn it in college." Sheeley has a bachelor's degree in agricultural science.

irrigation: ditch versus spray versus drip

Traditionally, California farmers have used ditch irrigation—water that is channeled through ditches along the sides of the crops. This year Ted Sheely installed a sprinkler irrigation system. Installation and aluminum pipes cost $100,000. But sprinklers use 20 percent less water than ditch irrigation. Sheely said he would have used drip irrigation, which uses half the water of ditch irrigation by distributing water in underground pipes with tiny holes. But installation costs between $1,100 and $1,200 an acre.

Probes set in the ground by the Westlands Water District monitor the air temperature, relative humidity, solar intensity, and the in-ground temperature. "We use it all summer," says Sheely. "It

Ted Sheely checks out water from his "monster well." The ditch will channel it to the field, where the water will be sprayed or fed through hoses to the crops.

tells us how irrigated the land is, and how much we need from the wells, so no water is wasted."

the ripper

Sheely suddenly swerves his truck across a field to check out his ripper. A ripper acts like a set of huge fingers that, pulled by a tractor, digs six feet into the ground and breaks up the clods of earth after the harvest. As a drought measure, it is highly cost-effective, Sheeley says. Breaking up the earth with deep cuts allows the rain that falls in the winter to sink into the earth to be stored there. It cost $160,000, but it might mean the difference between having a field with sufficient water to plant and not being able to grow a crop.

"If you have an edge, use it," says Sheeley. Besides, he likes the machine. "Three hundred and twenty-five-horsepower!" he says of the tractor. "Can you imagine three hundred and twenty-five horses pulling this thing across the field?"

the laser leveler

In the center of another field, a thin metal pole supports a rapidly spinning laser beam. It looks like a small lighthouse. The beam sends out a signal to a computer that is housed in a truck slowly circling the outer edge of the field, towing a leveler. "It costs three hundred dollars an acre for this," says Sheely. "What I own has to pay its own way." This hydraulic device makes the field absolutely level so there is no chance for any water to escape. The water goes straight down into the root zones, not into the paths between the fields.

the grinder

Across the road in another field, a machine is digging deep into the ruts left by the cotton harvest to cut up the leftovers of the cotton plant. Sheely explains that this will create a humus that will keep the soil moist, but most important, it will kill the roots so he can plant safflower next season, and rotate the crops. Sometimes farmers plant one crop in one field, then let it lie fallow for a season. Crop rotation, or varying the type of crop planted in a field, is good for the soil, because each crop uses different soil nutrients. During drought, crop rotation keeps the soil moist.

Killing the cotton root, Sheely says, also kills the food of a nasty insect called the pink boll weevil, which eats the cotton crops. This helps cut down on the use of pesticides, and periodically, during the growing season, a crop duster will fly low over the fields, releasing thousands of moths that will eat the boll weevils. Because the moths are sterile, they do not reproduce.

the ideal farm

Sheely says that diversifying what he grows is the only way to be sure to make a profit. "My ideal farm will have lots of uncontested water, with some cotton, yellow onions, sweet corn, tomatoes, maybe some pistachio trees. I used to grow watermelons," he remembers, "and my older son and I would drive out here just after the sun was up, and we'd cut open a watermelon that would still be cold from the night frost. It doesn't get any better than that."

future farms

He heads his truck back to his office and talks about the future of farming. Experts foresee more water marketing, whereby those who have water will sell it to those who do not. In the San Joaquin Valley, this means farmers will have the option of selling some of their water, or their land with surface water on it, to the city of Los Angeles. This will even out the distribution of water and create a fair price. This will also mean that farmers will have to cut back to smaller farms and will grow more vegetables and specialty crops like nut trees. There will be fewer cattle farms and fields of cattle feed. Small farmers who do not have good water supplies will have to sell their farms and do other things.

Drought for California farmers is a "one-more-year thing." Each measure they take against drought is like fighting little battles in a bigger war. The real problem is how much water of the state's supply they will be allowed to use.

on the leading edge

Drought is a different experience for farmers than for city dwellers, because it can ruin their lives. It's been said that farmers live as intensely in the present as astronauts on a mission or surfers in the belly of a roller: they can't afford to make any mistakes. Accidents with machinery or losing a crop to the weather are risks they have to live with day by day. "Water is like gold here," says Ted Sheely.

"Our water law is antiquated," he says. "It's been tried and tried in the courts. As the saying goes, 'Whiskey's for drinking, water's for fighting over.' But out of it, somehow we've molded a system that works."

freshwater from the ocean: desalination

The city of Santa Barbara, a few miles north of Los Angeles, on the same arid coastal zone, installed the largest reverse-osmosis desalination plant in the United States in 1992. A drought in 1989 had left the city's reservoirs so dry engineers drilled wells in them to find water. It was clear a new source of water needed to be found. Residents voted in favor of a desalination plant to have a dependable drought backup system. They also wanted to avoid legal disputes involving water rights.

Ionics, a company in Watertown, Massachusetts, designed, built, owns, and maintains the plant, which provides about 7,500 acre-feet of water that 190,000 residents buy.

There are three types of desalination processes: reverse osmosis, electrodialysis, and distillation, which is the type used on Antigua.

reverse osmosis

This is the cheapest and most widely used method. Long pipes bring in ocean water to the plant where the water is forced at a terrific pressure (like the miners' nozzles) against a filter that blocks out salts and impurities, leaving pure water. After it is purified, the water is piped out to the reservoirs. The salts and impurities are then distributed back into the ocean via another long pipe that deposits them several miles off the coast.

electrodialysis

This method works in the same way, using a filter to block out impurities, but it charges the water electrically. When the electrical charge is shot into the water, the salts and minerals coalesce into

REVERSE OSMOSIS DESALINATION

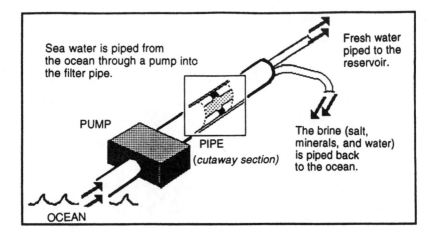

Sea water is piped from the ocean through a pump into the filter pipe.

Fresh water piped to the reservoir.

PUMP

PIPE
(cutaway section)

The brine (salt, minerals, and water) is piped back to the ocean.

OCEAN

Salt water is pumped at high pressure through the pipe. Fresh water is forced through the sides of a very fine filter without the salt and minerals.

PIPE DETAIL

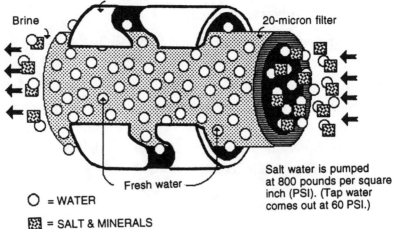

Brine

20-micron filter

Fresh water

Salt water is pumped at 800 pounds per square inch (PSI). (Tap water comes out at 60 PSI.)

○ = WATER

▨ = SALT & MINERALS

Reverse osmosis desalination.

solids. The water is then forced against a filter, and piped out into reservoirs. The salts are returned to the sea.

distillation

Used in Antigua, distillation is considered to be the most expensive system because it requires a lot of fuel to heat the water. It also is the most ancient form of desalination: Ancient Greek philosopher Aristotle advised sailors to do it at sea. Today, steam desalination is still used widely around the world, including in Saudi Arabia.

Worst-Case Drought: In the Sahel

Everyone has seen the pictures of the worst-case ravages of drought—children with empty eyes and bloated stomachs, women waiting in line for food, carrying cups and clutching dying babies, old men and women reaching out with thin arms, their faces describing the pain of hunger, of being sick and sad and helpless.

the sahel

Many of the pictures of starving people come from the African Sahel, an arid to semiarid band that separates the Sahara Desert in the north from the tropical rain forest in the south. The Sahel ranges from 60 to 135 miles wide (100 to 225 kilometers), and stretches about 5,000 miles (8,000 kilometers) across Africa from the Atlantic Ocean to the Red Sea.

Right in the middle of the Sahel is Lake Chad, once large

During a drought in Chad, a woman waits for an international relief agency plane to drop supplies of food.
National Oceanic and Atmospheric Administration.

enough to be called an inland ocean. Now shared by four countries—Niger, Nigeria, Chad, and Cameroun—the lake has been shrunk by drought to a quarter of its earlier size.

As far as anyone can remember, the drought of 1983–1984 in the Sahel was the worst in the region's history. International relief agencies sent 7 million tons of food to the area. Farmers had already eaten seeds they were saving to plant, and desperate mothers were cooking bitter leaves from trees to feed their children. In some places, hungry villagers lit fires to smoke rats out of bushes to have something to eat.

drought + poverty = famine

But drought was not the sole cause of the famine that killed hundreds of thousands of Africans. "Droughts don't cause famine," said one relief worker; "poverty does." Even in the driest times, imported food is usually available in village stores and in the marketplaces. But as the demand for food goes up, so do the prices; and only rich people can afford to buy it.

Small farmers whose crops have been wiped out by drought often have to sell their land to buy food, and then they have nothing. What usually happens then is that the men of the family go to the cities to try to find jobs as laborers or taxi drivers, and the women are left at home trying to grow enough food to keep their children and the older members of their family alive.

When relief food is flown into the country, relief vans often have difficulty getting to remote villages. Much of the Sahel, a severe drought area, is flat and treeless, too hot to travel in from noon until three o'clock. No roads connect the remote villages.

So the hungry must walk to the relief food centers. In drought and famine, adults and children, especially, who need protein and calories to grow, often become sick and weak, and the long, hot, and dusty trek to the food distribution center is a nightmare.

The Sahel region crosses nine or ten countries, but those countries include about three hundred different tribal groups, people with different customs and sometimes completely different languages. Some are farmers, and others are nomads who drive their cattle from grazing land to grazing land. Altogether, the population of the Sahel is thought to be about 116 million people who cope, for better or worse, with a dry to very dry climate.

Cattle herders also have a hard time. They drive their tired

These women in Burkina Faso, in the African Sahel, who have walked miles under a blazing sun from their tiny villages to a relief center, now wait in line to be able to get grain to feed their families. National Oceanic and Atmospheric Administration.

herds along the roads searching for a small patch of grass for food and a pond for water. In their search for a better place, they often migrate across political borders into other countries. But when they do find shallow water holes, they compete with increased populations of malaria-carrying mosquitoes and tsetse flies, also looking for water. These afflict not only the herders but the cattle. Carcasses of dead cattle, undernourished, dehydrated, and diseased, still litter roadsides in parts of the Sahel.

drought + war = famine

During a drought in countries where political power struggles result in wars, or where civil and tribal conflicts create guerrilla wars, as in Ethiopia, Somalia, and the Sudan, where every boy and every young and old man carries a gun, the whole society breaks down. Often the soldiers steal the relief food and sometimes wound or kill relief workers. But they don't steal the food to eat it. They steal it to gain an advantage in the warfare. Sometimes they just stockpile the food and later sell it at outrageous prices.

The result is that many people die, or become environmental refugees. The children who manage to survive not only starvation and dehydration, but the epidemics of measles, often suffer long-term physiological damage. And still the photographs that reach the rest of the world suggest that the problems were caused by drought.

Drought only makes existing conditions worse.

During drought, cattle carcasses like this litter the roads in the African Sahel. In East Africa, where many wild animals live, the first to die during drought are the herbivores—antelopes, giraffes, and zebras—because they rely on grass and leaves for food. The carnivores—lions, cheetahs, and leopards—catch them more easily then because they are weak and dying. The scavengers— hyenas, jackals, and vultures—survive by picking clean the bones that the carnivores leave. National Oceanic and Atmsopheric Administration.

rain: maybe

One of the problems is that rainfall in the Sahel is so variable and so undependable that before each growing season, Nigerian government officials ask villagers to fast and to pray for rain. The rainy season, roughly from June to September, can vary from 120 to 140 days, and rainfall ranges anywhere from 20 to 48 inches (48 to 122 centimeters). Evaporation takes about 80 percent of that water back to the skies.

the winds

Exactly where the rain falls depends on the winds. Because the Sahel is close to the equator, the winds blowing out of the northern hemisphere meet the winds blowing out of the southern hemisphere. In good years the meeting of the winds happens over the Sahel and creates an updraft that produces clouds that carry rain. But in some years the winds coming from the north out of the Sahara are so strong that they keep the winds from the south far below the region, so that the rains never reach the Sahel.

a warm atlantic ocean

Climatologists think other forces are at work in Sahel droughts. Droughts in the past ten to twenty years appear to have been made worse by a rise in the surface temperature of the Atlantic Ocean—not unlike the El Niño in the Pacific. This rise in sea surface temperature also causes abnormal rains in Brazil, on the other side of the Atlantic. This might be linked to the El Niño event in the Pacific, or it might be part of a larger system of weather—as yet undiscovered—that causes *both* oceans to heat up.

a moving desert?

A few years ago scientists thought the Sahara was moving south into the Sahel, swallowing up green things and turning them into sand. But several years of satellite observations produced some interesting pictures:

- From 1980 to 1984, the Sahara moved south 144 miles (240 kilometers).
- From 1984 to 1985, it moved north 66 miles (110 kilometers).

Satellite pictures of the continent of Africa. The one on the left was taken in March 1989; the one on the right, in October 1989. In the Sahel region, the darker gray just below the light gray of the Sahara Desert, drought extends across almost the whole width of the continent during the dry season in the picture on the left. A long region of drought still exists during the rainy season in the picture on the right. Lake Chad is the dark spot in the middle of the Sahel. NASA Headquarters Earth Sciences and Applications Division.

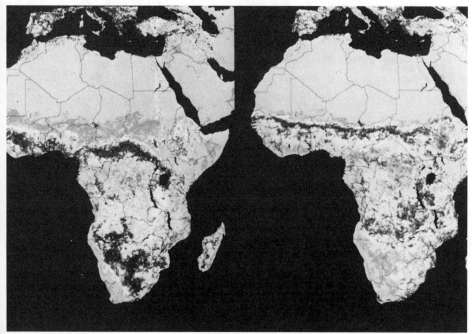

- In 1986, it moved north 18 miles (30 kilometers).
- In 1987, it moved south 33 miles (55 kilometers).
- In 1988, it moved north 60 miles (100 kilometers).
- In 1989 to 1990, it moved south 46 miles (77 kilometers).

The winds do blow the Sahara sands around. Some have been found as far away as Brazil, and over long periods, some sands have accumulated into dunes outside villages in the Sahel.

the difference between deserts and desertification

But the Sahara is not overtaking the Sahel. The chief problem in the Sahel is desertification: the soil is overworked, exposed to the sun, dried out, and whipped up by the winds. Trees are cut down for firewood. The problem is man-made, and droughts hurry it along. In some parts of the Sahara, cutting down trees encouraged some desertification, but the vast sands of the Sahara are the result of thousands of years of lack of rain.

In the Sahel country of Niger, peanuts were grown as a cash crop, to be exported to make money. Being able to sell something that is in demand is a good way to bring money into a poor country. But the project got out of hand. With foreign-aid loans, farmers bought tractors so they could plow up more and more acres to plant more to harvest more to export more.

Traditional farmers—those whose tribal fathers have been farming for centuries in the same place—always let some land lie fallow, without being planted for a season, so it can reabsorb nutrients. But when the same crop is planted year after year in the same fields, the soil loses its nutrients and can't hold moisture. Soon the

Cattle, goats, and sheep, pictured here with some horses and donkeys trying to keep cool under a tree in the midday sun, are numerous in the African Sahel region. Because they eat away the grass, plants, and shrubs wherever they are, they contribute to desertification, a condition in which the soil that has lost its vegetation has nothing to anchor it. In drought, the soil dries out and blows away. National Oceanic and Atmospheric Administration.

crops won't take root, and the topsoil blows away. This is desertification.

The Sahel has always had cattle. For hundreds of years, the Fulani people have kept herds of cattle, each one of which they know and call by name, because they believe cattle, like men, have souls. In Nigeria the Fulani herders have worked in harmony with farmers of the Kanuri people. The Kanuri let the Fulani cattle graze on their fallow fields. The cattle eat the weeds and fertilize the fields. The herders also give the farmers milk, and in return, the farmers give the herders grains.

But when all the fields are used to grow peanuts, they never lie fallow and the cattle get pushed off. The cattle herders then are forced to drive their herds many miles away onto abandoned farm fields, where scrub bushes hold the soil in place. The cattle eat away that vegetation, and the winds blow away still more soil.

Is this abuse or adaptation? You could argue that it is a way of adapting to a bad situation. Farmers adapt to modern methods to grow bigger crops to sell to avoid poverty. Herders adapt by moving their cattle to unused lands to keep their cattle alive to avoid poverty.

Camels, people, goats, sheep, horses, donkeys, and any wild animals that still live in the bush must share water from small ponds like this one in Chad, in the African Sahel. Without rain, the ponds shrink. Then people and animals must compete for water. National Oceanic and Atmospheric Administration.

But the soil is abused, and after a couple of years, tractors lie unrepaired in fields that are too dry to plant or to support enough grass to feed cattle.

Does the short-term gain justify the long-term abuse?

drought = man + nature

Some scientists see droughts in the Sahel as a giant network of climate change and man-made problems.

As vegetation is removed in overfarming and overgrazing, the albedo, or reflective quality of the land surface, is increased, and more sunlight is reflected back into space. Because less heat is held in the earth, the surface temperature becomes lower, and that reduces the possibility of making clouds.

No clouds: no rain.

one strange lake: lake chad

Despite the fact it is famous for drought, the Sahel has one of the most interesting bodies of water in the world—Lake Chad.

Here farmers take over the lake bed when the lake is low. The ground is rich and moist and good for growing crops. This is called *falling-flood farming,* and it is a coping method during drought.

a tradition of drought

Farmers have been planting the dry lake bed for a long time because the Sahel has a long history of droughts. Ancient sand dunes have even been found under Lake Chad. Between 1738 and

A palace guard from the kingdom of Borno in Nigeria near Lake Chad, about 120 years ago.
Gustave Nachtigal. *Sahara et Soudan* (Paris, Hachette, 1881).

1756, fifty thousand people were said to have died in the city of Timbuktu in Mali in a drought that lasted for eighteen years. Elders in Nigeria still remember a year-long drought in 1913, during which entire villages perished.

For centuries Lake Chad was a meeting place where traders who caravanned across the Sahara Desert met traders who carried goods up from the rest of Africa. Sahel means *coast* in Arabic, and the Sahel is the coast of the great desert. Like freighters crossing the ocean, the Sahara traders, with thousands of camels, brought in everything from salt to silk brocades from the Middle East, the Mediterranean, and Europe. From Africa came traders loaded with indigo cloth, gold, kola nuts, leopard skins, and smoked meat and fish.

In towns on the lakeshore, traders stocked up on water and food, haggled over prices, and stayed up far into the night gossiping and telling stories.

If they had brought royal gifts of Arabian horses, they would call at the palace of the King of Borno, near Lake Chad. Borno, in present-day Nigeria, was the largest kingdom in central Africa. The king was so rich, it was said, even his dogs wore collars of gold. Once a year, his people entertained him with dazzling horse shows, with acrobats and horse races, wrestling, dancing, and storytelling.

Traders no longer network the Sahara to Lake Chad, and the lake is a fraction of the size it used to be. It measured 13,800 square miles (23,000 square kilometers) in 1963, but only 1,200 square miles (2,000 square kilometers) in 1985.

But is drought really turning this great lake into a pond?

Weird and strange Lake Chad is full of surprises.

For a long time, it was barely mentioned in Western history

More than a hundred years ago, a German explorer crossed the Sahara Desert on one of the old trade routes to the Kingdom of Borno and Lake Chad. In this drawing made from his report, an elephant bathes on the lakeshore. Gustave Nachtigal. *Sahara et Soudan* (Paris, Hachette, 1881)

books, because early African explorers came back with completely different stories. One explorer risked his life crossing the Sahara in search of what he thought was an inland ocean, only to arrive at a time when the lake had shrunk. Tired, angry, and disappointed, he described it as "a puddle."

A few years later, another explorer took pictures of huge waves crashing against the lake's shores. One mapmaker gave up, calling Lake Chad's shifting outline "a nightmare."

Scientists now know that the lake, like the earth's weather systems, is subject to long-term, short-term, and local changes. Winds and the lunar tidal pulls affect its shape, too, which drives mapmakers mad. In 1905, for example, it seemed to be a swamp; and four years later, in 1909, it was a hefty lake.

But the strangest thing is that it shrinks to half its size *every year*, and that is during the *rainy* season. This is because Lake Chad gets most of its water from the Chari-Logone rivers that come up from Cameroun, south of the lake. But the rivers in Cameroun don't fill up with water until *after* the rainy season is over. Then they begin to move the water north into the lake. At that time, between October and December—officially the dry season—the river water fills the lake, which expands rapidly and covers the hundreds of acres of its lake bed in water that is fifteen feet deep. So the lake is there only during the dry season.

Rich in phytoplankton, the lake is home to hundreds of fish, frogs, mollusks, and crocodiles. In the dry season, fishermen paddle their long pirogues across the lake, pulling in fish for market. Snakes wriggle and writhe through the reeds on the banks,

Fishermen use long wooden, flat-bottomed boats on Lake Chad that are like those used a hundred years ago. Today they use outboard motors.

and legend says that a six-foot perch, which the local people call the Elephant of the Water, lives there.

the lake chad farmers

The lake is a savior not only to fishermen but to farmers.

During the worst of the drought in 1983–1984, the farmers in the Lake Chad region did what their fathers had done before, and their fathers before them: they moved onto the lake bed during the rainy season and farmed the rich, moist soil that is exposed for six months of the year.

During the drought in 1984, an estimated 25,000 people from all over Nigeria joined the local farmers on the lake bed, built temporary houses out of millet stalks, and set up refrigerators with generators powered by their trucks.

During the year of the worst drought known to memory, when thousands were dying, the Lake Chad farmers survived. Only lack of enough trucks to transport their crops prevented the farmers from selling their goods to those who were starving.

Each year, until the lake comes back in the dry season, farmers grow maize, cowpeas, peanuts, barley, rice, okra, legumes, and other produce in their giant public garden. At harvest, you can see men carrying goods to market in two-wheeled carriages pulled by lyre-horned cattle or in trucks that gouge great ruts in the lake bed road. One man wearing a fez and Ray-Bans deftly negotiates his motor scooter through the truck ruts as he transports a mountainous load of greens tied onto the back.

After the lake comes back, the farmers plant what they need in their fields surrounding it.

government improvement projects

Lake Chad farmers wouldn't give it up for the world.

A few years ago, when government officials became alarmed at the frequency of droughts, they instituted a new farm program for much of the area around Lake Chad.

Most of the traditional farmers around the lake rely on rain to grow their food during the rainy season. In drought years, when it doesn't rain, they suffer.

The new government program invested a lot of money in spray irrigation using water from aquifers and moved whole villages onto empty farmland. But the sun evaporated most of the spray before it reached the crops, the crops were slow to grow,

Engineer Usman Sandabe stands at the sluice of one of the canals built to direct some of the lake water into the fields. During drought, however, the lake shrinks back from the canals.

and, when the irrigation arms broke, no one knew how to repair them.

So the farmers went back to their original rain-fed farms.

Then the government built a long canal into Lake Chad, with pumping stations and channels to bring the water into ditches to irrigate the farmlands. But Lake Chad shrank the year the canal was built, and the canal fell uselessly short of the water. When farmers needed it most, the water did not come.

So government officials went back to their offices and held meetings to discuss how to raise more money to engage engineers to build a longer canal that would reach securely into the lake.

While they planned, the farmers went back to the lake bed.

sources of water

Lake Chad might have another surprise, too.

Most of the water around Lake Chad comes from government wells dug into aquifers. Part of the Lake Chad government project was to dig more wells, many of them near the villages. This makes it a lot easier for the women, who used to spend as many as seven hours a day walking to common water sources. Now they can go to their village well several times a day, pulling up the bucket and spilling the water into their big clay urns, which they will carry on one arm, while balancing a baby on the other.

The government also dug boreholes, tubes sunk into the deep aquifer, powered by diesel pumps that bring up gushing geysers of water, creating muddy ponds. These become beehives of activity, with herders bringing in their thirsty cattle, children playing water games, and truckers and mechanics trading gossip in voices loud enough to be heard above the roar of the diesel pump.

Before the government dug village wells, women walked several miles a day to community wells in larger villages for water. Sometimes they went twice a day.

In some communities, tanker trucks load up water from boreholes, then drive through the streets of the bigger towns and sell it. A study found that the average household buys two buckets, or about twenty gallons per person per day, and spends an amazing 18 percent of its income on water.

the secret of lake chad

The point is, a suspicious amount of water exists around Lake Chad, filling the wells and gushing abundantly out of boreholes.

Yet the lake has been shrinking.

Another strange thing about the lake is its lack of salt. Most old land-bound lakes collect salt over the years. The Great Salt Lake in Utah, for example, has so much salt in it that it is saltier than the ocean.

Where is Lake Chad's salt going?

Solomon Isiorho is a Nigerian hydrogeologist who studied in the United States, and then went back to Lake Chad. He had a theory that the salt that should have been in the lake was seeping through the ground under the lake into the aquifers. And if the salt was seeping into the aquifers, Isiorho wondered if the lake was secretly storing its water underground.

Was the lake *leaking*?

Assisted by geology students from the local university, Isiorho first tested the water in the wells that was coming up from the aquifers. They found salt and other residues that indicated that a lot of the missing water in Lake Chad, so disguised by its shifting size and shape-changing, is safely stored in the aquifer below. It turns out that Lake Chad's seepage rate—the amount of water that goes into the ground—is a very high 20 percent.

But how big is this water bank? To try to map its underground and invisible boundaries, Isiorho and the students set up a resistivity meter on one of the canals several miles from the lakeshore. Wires connected the meter to metal stakes (about three feet, or one meter, long) driven into the ground. These shot an electrical charge deep into the earth that registers on the meter.

In the vast uninhabited flat lands around Lake Chad, clumps of trees across the fields signal a village. Each village has a well outside its walls. Here, villagers help draw up water for testing. High salt content might indicate that waters from Lake Chad are stored in one of the aquifers.

While their fathers and brothers and uncles help test the water, the kids dance and play on the village tower.

Working from dawn until noon, when the sun became unbearable, Isiorho and the students covered several miles, driving in the stakes, sending down the pulse. When the meter reader called out the number, another would record it. Then the team would move on.

From the meter readings, Isiorho was able to construct a kind of underground map. From it, he could identify the presence of underground water and cracks in the rock, which might contain water. By the end of the summer, Isiorho believed he had enough data to say that Lake Chad had somehow managed to store a huge amount of water in the aquifers, enough so that this area in the Sahel might never have to be bothered by drought again.

If government officials and scientists working together can come up with a plan that will safely tap the vast pool of under-ground water around the lake without collapsing the aquifers, and build an economical water delivery and storage system, there will be enough water for drinking, for farms, and for cattle—enough to keep away the sting of famine.

a case of adaptation

Social scientists say that in severe droughts, people adapt, migrate, or die. In the Sahel, people have done all of these. But migration and death have come not directly from drought, but from poverty and war.

Where people could fight drought alone, they did.

Each year people survive what is called the Hungry Season, a period just before the harvest, when all of the stored food is used up. Food supplies are short, and prices in stores are high. Because people aren't getting enough calories, they are vulnerable to dis-ease. Pregnant women usually lose their babies at this time.

This has made farmers in the Sahel tough. Traditions of drought and Hungry Seasons have taught them how to cope dur-ing hard times.

They have a long history of adaptation.

storytelling

In the villages when the moon is growing full, villagers around Lake Chad stay outside and tell stories. Sitting in a circle in the glow of the moonlight, they take turns, recounting favorite legends, myths, or stories they've read in school.

One night one of the Kanuri farmer elders told the story of the first people to come to the lake. Called the So, they were giants who built big towns, knew how to make things out of metal, and were ruled by kings and queens. Their voices were so loud, it was said, one person could talk to another in a neighboring town. They were so big one hunter could carry back a whole elephant on his shoulders. They could build huge dams on the rivers in one day, and turn the flow of the rivers from south to north.

But despite the fact they knew how to dam the rivers, over the years they had to adapt to drought. What happened to the So?

"The So did not go anywhere," the elder said. "They died here. They could not get water, and gradually the people gave birth to smaller and smaller people. This happened because of lack of water. The So people became Kanuri."

EARTH'S WATER

On Earth, 97 percent of all the water is

SALT WATER

Only 3 percent is

FRESH WATER

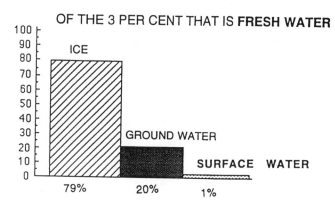

OF THE 3 PER CENT THAT IS **FRESH WATER**

ICE — 79%
GROUND WATER — 20%
SURFACE WATER — 1%

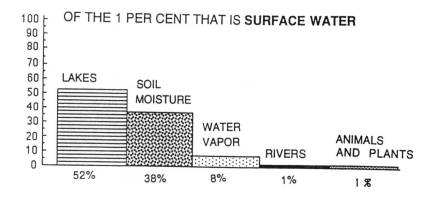

OF THE 1 PER CENT THAT IS **SURFACE WATER**

LAKES — 52%
SOIL MOISTURE — 38%
WATER VAPOR — 8%
RIVERS — 1%
ANIMALS AND PLANTS — 1%

Water Use: When Is It Too Much?

Brushing your teeth: If you leave the water running and you're in a hurry, you may use up two to five gallons.

If you leave the water running while you do an exceptionally thorough job, or just daydream, you use ten to twenty gallons.

If you brush your teeth using water in a glass, you use less than one quart.

A bath: The average bathtub holds twenty-five to thirty gallons of water.

A shower: This depends on the showerhead. Some use six to twelve gallons a minute, so a fifteen-minute shower uses 90 to 180 gallons. A low-flow showerhead sends out only 2.5 gallons a minute, which means a fifteen-minute shower uses 37.5 gallons.

Flushing the toilet: The standard toilet uses six to seven gallons per flush. Putting a plastic jug filled with water in the tank

We suffer if we lose one tenth
of our body's water, or 9.5 pounds
of a 150-pound person.

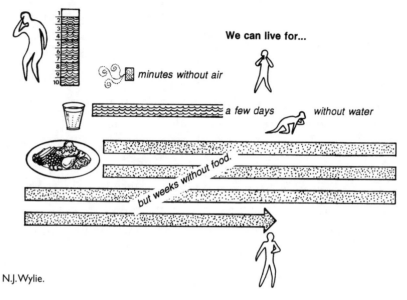

We can live for...

minutes without air

a few days without water

but weeks without food.

N.J. Wylie.

brings that amount down to four gallons a flush. An ultra low-flow
toilet uses 1.6 gallons per flush.

Washing a car: Using a hose consumes about fifty gallons of
water to wash and rinse the average-size car. Sponging the car with
a bucket of water takes about fifteen gallons.

Watering a garden: Watering a small garden for ten minutes
with a hose uses about eighty gallons of water.

(To convert gallons to liters, multiply by 3.7.)

polluted water

Some of the earth's 3 percent supply of freshwater is lost to pollution. Dead, bloated fish float in green slime against rutted river-

banks or lakeshores. They have been killed by pollutants in the water. Pollutants come from industrial waste and from everyday things like human and animal waste, phosphates from laundry detergents, and nitrates from fertilizers.

These chemicals collect in rivers and lakes and lead to what's called *eutrophication*. This is the condition that results when algae feed on nitrates and phosphates, multiply in large numbers, and then die, giving off carbon dioxide. Dead algae produce algae bloom, a green smelly slime. Because the oxygen in the water is used up, the rivers and lakes do not support life.

Agriculture consumes about 75 percent of all the freshwater in the world, and it is the biggest source of organic waste, not only from humans, but from animals and harvested crops. Pesticides and herbicides leach into streams and rivers, as well as into the groundwater. In areas where trees have been cut down, agricultural waste runs off into the ocean.

purifying wastewater

Much of this wastewater can be turned into drinking water in treatment plants. There are three types of treatment plants:

- *Primary* wastewater treatment plants operate mechanically and remove sediments from the water.
- *Secondary* wastewater plants biologically remove organic matter and bacteria.
- *Tertiary* wastewater plants remove hazardous matter both biologically and chemically, by adding chlorine and other chemicals to the water. Most of the drinking water in developed countries comes from tertiary plants.

WHY DOES THE BODY NEED WATER ?

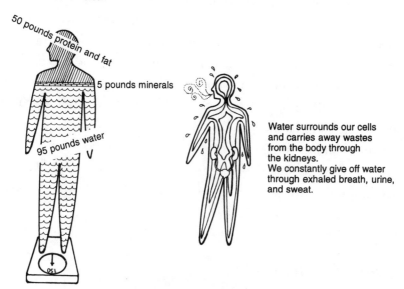

150 - Pound Person

50 pounds protein and fat

5 pounds minerals

95 pounds water

Water surrounds our cells
and carries away wastes
from the body through
the kidneys.
We constantly give off water
through exhaled breath, urine,
and sweat.

Without water, a person first feels very thirsty.
Then his lips and tongue will be dry.
His heartrate will increase. His breathing
will become very rapid. If he continues without water, the person
will become dizzy and confused. He will imagine
he sees water. Finally, he will fall into a coma.

Rehydration means the replacement of lost
fluids.   It is accomplished by drinking water
or by receiving fluids intravenously.   N.J.Wylie.

The Clean Water Act, passed by the U.S. Congress in 1972,
was intended to upgrade sewage treatment plants to make rivers
and streams safe for fishing and swimming.

But in many parts of the world, water from wells and water
from reservoirs are untreated. Human waste often contaminates
drinking water and multiplies the germs that produce cholera,

typhoid fever, and diarrhea. Infant diarrhea is widespread in many parts of the world, and many babies die from it. In addition, the cure for these diseases requires a lot of water to rehydrate the body. Often, the problems simply continue unchecked.

Industrial waste is the source of many chemicals and heavy metals, such as mercury, lead, cadmium, and zinc. These are either not biodegradable, or take a very long time to degrade. When factories flush them into rivers and streams, they also leach into the soil or run off into the ocean. Some chemicals last forever: DDT and PCBs were banned in the 1970s, but traces of these chemicals are still found in deep-ocean fish.

Another source of pollution for oceans, rivers, and lakes is sulphur and nitrogen oxide air emissions from the burning of coal and oil, which fall as acid rain.

ocean pollution

Oceans would seem to be so huge that they cannot be subject to pollution. But acid rain, runoff containing silt and pesticides from farms, and chemicals and heavy metals from industry wind up in the ocean. So do trash, oil, and gasoline from ships and boats, and toxic waste, some of it radioactive. Oil spills from tanker accidents take years to clean. All of this affects wildlife habitats, coastal wetlands, coral reefs, and mangrove swamps, and it contaminates the plankton that fish eat—and humans eat the fish.

Excessive amounts of dead plankton release excessive amounts of carbon dioxide into the atmosphere. This collects in the greenhouse band, which contributes to a rise in global temperature, which then changes weather patterns, giving rise to more droughts.

Most experts believe that some water pollution can be

reversed. Over time, polluted lakes can be flushed out. Experiments with green algae and bacteria have been found to break down chemicals in water. Some plants, such as water hyacinth, seem to be miraculous in their ability to absorb heavy metals in water. Scientists don't yet understand how they do it.

But the two most important factors in keeping water systems healthy are:

- Conserving fresh water
- Preventing contaminants from entering water systems

This requires *management* of water use in communities: on farms, in households, and in industry. Very few communities around the world do this.

urban conservation

California has more than two hundred wastewater reclamation plants that recycle water from industry, restaurants, car washes, and so on. Partially purified, the water is considered safe enough to use for irrigation in landscaping and wildlife habitats.

Throughout the state, water-saving, low-flow plumbing devices are installed in all new construction. Water meters monitor water use in houses and apartment buildings, and landlords and homeowners are fined if they use more than their allotment. Some cities ban car washing and lawn watering altogether. Other cities allow it only on certain days of the week.

gray water

Households in a lot of communities are recycling their sink, shower and bath, laundry, and dishwashing water. This is called gray water. It can be used to water lawns and wash cars. But bacteria collect quickly, so gray water should not be allowed to sit around. It should never be used if someone in the household has a contagious disease. Households that use gray water should make sure they use phosphate-free laundry detergents.

gardens

Many homeowners are replanting their gardens with plants that grow wild in their own area, because those plants are already adapted to local water conditions.

In very dry areas, many homeowners use *xeriscaping* (from the Greek, *xeros*, which means dry). This involves planting drought-resistant plants like lavender, daisies, and poppies. Because it is estimated that a twenty- by forty-foot green lawn requires 2,500 gallons of water a month (or the amount a family of four could use in ten days), some homeowners are giving up green lawns for brick or concrete walkways, or local ground-covering plants.

the future

Some scientists say that water will replace oil as the most important resource in the twenty-first century. Population explosions, farm irrigation, and environmental needs are all increasing.

Because rainfall is not the same every day in every place, some scientists foresee storing water in underground water banks, from which it can be drawn out when droughts threaten. Ideally, pipes would be laid all around the world, so that areas with a lot of water could share it with areas with less water.

But distribution is a political problem. Who decides what community gets how much? Someone has to monitor the withdrawals of water. Would some communities be able to draw "interest" if they used less than their allotment? Bank robbers have been in business as long as there have been banks. Would there be water robbers? Water terrorists?

the ideal water community

The ideal water community would pump some of its water from aquifers and some from rainwater stored in clean and covered reservoirs.

Industries would keep contaminating chemicals in closed systems and would purify and recycle their used water.

Farmers would use drip irrigation, pipes buried in the ground that give off a minimum but steady input of water to plants. With drip irrigation, nothing is lost to evaporation. Farmers would also use high-tech farming techniques to make sure they were not using too much water. Farms would use natural herbicides and keep farmland drained to prevent salinization of the soil. Ocean desalination plants would be driven by wind or solar power to replace power sources that need to burn fossil fuels to generate energy.

Community water commissioners would make sure everybody was conserving water and preventing pollution. Each household would collect and recycle its own gray water. Homeowners would plant gardens with plants that grow naturally in the area. Timers on faucets would limit water output.

Clean water would be preserved and protected for wildlife in rivers and streams and in wetlands. Communities would replant trees where they have been cut down.

Beach hotels would use their own desalination plants for water for tourists.

The fact remains that the human body needs two liters of water a day to stay healthy. And everybody on earth is entitled to those two liters.

Resource List

Weather Modification Association
P.O. Box 8116
Fresno, CA 93747

Ocean Drilling Program
1000 Discovery Drive
Texas A&M University
College Station, TX 77845-9547

Consortium for International Earth Science
    Information Network
CIESIN
1968 Green Road
P.O. Box 134003
Ann Arbor, MI 48113

Water Education Foundation
717 H Street, Suite 517
Sacramento, CA 95814

Jet Propulsion Laboratory
4800 Oak Grove Drive
Mail Stop 300-323
Pasadena, CA 91109

Hydrometeorological Information Center
Office of Hydrology
National Weather Service
National Oceanic and Atmospheric
    Administration
1325 East-West Highway #7116
Silver Spring, MD 20910

United Nations Environmental Program
UNEP Regional Office for North America
UNDC Two Building
Room 0803
Two United Nations Plaza
New York, NY 10017

National Center for Atmospheric Research
P.O. Box 3000
Boulder, CO 80307-3000

Environmental Awareness Group
P.O. Box 103
St. John's
Antigua, West Indies

U.S.D.A. Soil Conservation Service
7515 N.E. Ankeny Road
Ankeny, IA 50021-9764

Index